UNDERNEATH

A NOVEL BY BONNABELLE GOODRUM

© 11/30/2013, Bonnabelle Goodrum

I dedicate this book to those who believed me when I told them I was writing a book.

TABLE OF CONTENTS:

PART 1-THE CITY

CHAPTER 1: THE PURE CITY-PAGE 6

CHAPTER 2: NIGHTMARE ON SHIMMER STREET-PAGE 16

CHAPTER 3: A VISIT TO THE DOCTOR-PAGE 21

CHAPTER 4: HANNAH-PAGE 28

CHAPTER 5: HANNAH'S HOME-PAGE 34

CHAPTER 6: FORGETTING-PAGE 43

CHAPTER 7: ROBBED-PAGE 54

CHAPTER 8: SHOULD I STAY OR SHOULD I GO-PAGE 63

CHAPTER 9: HOME IS WHERE THE DEATH IS-PAGE 65

CHAPTER 10: NEW HOME-PAGE 72

CHAPTER 11: VIVID DREAMER-PAGE 78

CHAPTER 12: I WAS KIDDING-PAGE 81

CHAPTER 13: PANCAKES AND MYSTERY-PAGE 84

CHAPTER 14: FUGITIVES-PAGE 88

CHAPTER 15: LEGENDS AND STORIES-PAGE 90

CHAPTER 16: THE SECOND DAY-PAGE 102

CHAPTER 17: WASTING ENERGY-PAGE 104

CHAPTER 18: SIGNAL-PAGE 107

CHAPTER 19: BETRAYAL-PAGE 111

CHAPTER 20: CAUGHT-PAGE 116

CHAPTER 21: PRISON-PAGE 118

CHAPTER 22: TRIAL-PAGE 122

CHAPTER 23: TRANSPORT-PAGE 126

PART 2- THE GLOAM

CHAPTER 24: LIFE IN THE GLOAM-PAGE 138

CHAPTER 25: IN THE BELLY OF THE BEAST-PAGE 147

CHAPTER 26: OTTO-PAGE 153

CHAPTER 27: NIGHTMARES IN A NIGHTMARE-PAGE 159

CHAPTER 28: OTTO THE JERK-PAGE 161

CHAPTER 29: MISTAKE-PAGE 163

CHAPTER 30: CHAMBER OF DEATH-PAGE 168

CHAPTER 31: CIVILIZATION IN THE DARKNESS-PAGE 171

CHAPTER 32: REUNION-PAGE 174

CHAPTER 33: DEATH SIMULATORS EVERYWHERE-PAGE 176

CHAPTER 34: LOST AND FOUND-PAGE 191

CHAPTER 35: EYE CAM-PAGE 195

CHAPTER 36: ENCAMPMENT OF ENEMIES-PAGE 199

CHAPTER 37: UP A TREE-PAGE 206

CHAPTER 38: KATIE-PAGE 212

CHAPTER 39: A LAST BREATH-PAGE 215

CHAPTER 40: MYSTERIOUS ENTERTAINMENT-PAGE 218

CHAPTER 41: OPPOSITES-PAGE 220

CHAPTER 42: TEST-PAGE 223

CHAPTER 43: TICKING TIME BOMB-PAGE 226

CHAPTER 44: DISINTEGRATED-PAGE 236

CHAPTER 45: WOODEN HOUSE-PAGE 238

CHAPTER 46: UNLOCKED-PAGE 242

CHAPTER 47: DAYDREAMER-PAGE 246

CHAPTER 48: MEET THE MAKER-PAGE 251

PART 1- THE CITY

CHAPTER 1: THE PURE CITY

We were running. I couldn't see much of anything; all that I could see was smoke. I heard someone shout for help, but I was too small to help them. What can a 7 year old girl do to help a woman shot in the stomach? The woman holding my hand stopped abruptly and started yelling. I couldn't hear much, my ear was still ringing from the explosions. It sounded like she was saying, "George! No! WHAT ARE YOU DOING?!" She screamed. I didn't know who George was, but something told me I didn't want to know what happened to him. The woman started talking to me, but I couldn't hear what she was saying. Then I saw her evaporate right before my eyes...

I woke up in a cold sweat, gasping for air. I looked around. "None of it was real, Perrie. You're safe….you're safe." I said. I got out of my sleeping tube and looked at myself in the mirror. "You really could lose some weight." I said, grabbing some pudge in my stomach. I wasn't the thinnest of the all and my thighs didn't have a gap, but I felt this was how I was supposed to be. My dark brown hair looked muddy blonde today. I went into the bathroom and started talking to the mirror.

"Good morning, Perrie. You look tired. Perhaps I could be of service?" She said with her elegant voice.

"Mirror, I want my eyes to look blue and my hair to look dark brown." I said. She made a few buzzing noises.

"I cannot make your eyes blue for the reason that you are of Asian descent. I can make colored contacts for you if that will please you. I am out of hair color dye, also." She said.

"I can live without them, and that's okay."

"You can live without your eyes? Confirm surgery."

"NO. I MEANT I CAN LIVE WITHOUT THE COLORED CONTACTS."

"Confirmed, color contacts destroyed."

I personally don't like the robots. It's the only thing I can't stand about our houses in The Pure City. I went to my bedside table and picked up the glass image of mother and father. "You are safe now." I said. Tears welled up in my eyes as I looked at Stella. She never deserved that reduction of time. It wasn't even her fault! She could never hurt someone. She was only 4. "I love you all and I know you're okay. It comforts me to know you can never be a victim of the disappearances that have been happening lately." I said. The disappearances are the name the citizens of The Pure City have given to the mysterious crimes that have been occurring lately. People have Light cards. Light cards determine how long you have to live. Everyone's Light card has at least 50,000 days on it. If you commit a crime, your days are automatically set to 0 and you are taken by the Officials to be put to rest. If you perform an offense, depending on how bad the offense is, you get at least 10 days taken away from you. My little sister, Stacy, was accused of committing a crime and was put to rest. I can't say anything about it, or else I will have days taken away. I should be thankful for what I have though. I live in a beautiful paradise of crystals! Everyone is happy. I must be happy…

The disappearances are happening more than they ever have before. Every day people go away. I don't know where or how, but they seem to just vanish! Ms. Ira lives just down the lane. She is getting into her days of rest, but I saw her light card! She had 39 days left. Yesterday, she, and her pet dog, went missing! She was such a nice elderly woman. She would sit for hours scrunched up in her chair, reading a book. I would take care of her dog, Max, when she took her annual celebratory vacation; (this is provided by The Pure City for every citizen.) She gave me cookies when I would bring him home. She would never get involved with the wrong people. She was smart. I don't understand why she disappeared.

I decided to get dressed in my favorite outfit: my navy blue and white ¾ baseball shirt, black jeans, white and black sneakers, and my gray hair bow. I stepped outside and smelled the fresh air. The Pure City has such a wonderful scent. I could sniff the smell of Powdered Popcorn to the right, the odor of the sea to the left. This is such a beautiful city. I walked down the lane to Sheer Roadway and took a left. I was in The Square. The Square is the center of The Pure City. This is where venders convene to sell their goods, others to find love and still others to admire this kingdom of elegance. I come here to sit under my favorite tree and read books. Today was different though, not many people were here. I would usually watch everyone and their doings…. but it was so empty you could hear a needle drop. I looked at my Light card. It lit up and showed my light bulb. The light bulb was pretty much full.

"47,900 days left." I said. 131 years sounds about right to me! If I last that long…..

 "Oh Perrie, you're fine. Everyone is most likely still asleep. It is 8:30 a.m. after all…." I said. I talk to myself too much.

I decided to run back home to grab a book and read in my favorite spot, even if no one was at The

Square for me to watch. The T.V. came on and started to speak.

"Attention citizens of The Pure City, the Officials are recharging your sparks for the day, please standby."

I almost forgot about my spark! Our sparks define who we are. Our spark is our trait. Each flicker of light is different. At the end of the day our sparks run out of electricity, and we get extremely tired. We return our sparks to the Officials, and they charge them for us. The spark gives us new traits every day. The Officials want us to live as many lives as we can before our days run out. When our Light cards run out of days, our spark burns out forever, and the traits we died with are never redistributed to another person.

I heard a knock on my door. I answered it. In front of me was a holographic message with a package attached to it. When I opened it up, the hologram showed an official.

"Perrie Fawn. Your spark is recharged. We hope you enjoy your traits for today."

Inside the package was my spark. It looked as beautiful as ever. It was like a light you could hold;

when you touched it, it would sparkle. I went to the mirror.

"Awake." I said.

"How may I help you Ms. Fawn?" She said.

"I have my spark."

"Do you need assistance installing it?"

"I only need your authorization to open the gate in my heart."

"I will do so."

Every time we input our spark, we need an authorization from our guardian to open the gate that was implanted into our hearts. When we first came to The Pure City, everyone was required to have a heart gate installed. We install the spark into the gate. The sparks give us the traits that make up our true selves. I felt a whirring in my chest. The gate was open. I touched the spark to my chest, and it sunk into my body. I felt its warmth and happiness. I had good traits today. I decided to go ahead with my plans to grab a book and read under my favorite tree in The Square. I quickly went downstairs into my library and picked out my only book I had. It was a book filled with fairytales from a long time ago. This was the only book anyone could have. Heck, it was the only book available in the city! I paid my whole entire sweets collection for this book. I had saved any kind of sweet I could find, and slowly paid off the book keeper, Mara. I went downstairs, out the door, down the lane and took a left at Sheer Roadway. I was back in the beautiful Square. There were a few people there. At least it wasn't empty like earlier…

I saw Jerome, the local farmer setting up his stand.

"Hey Perrie!" He yelled. Oh great, here we go again.

"Hey Jerome!" I called, forcing a smile.

"Ah, hello Perrie! I was wondering when you would show up."

"Actually, I was here at 8:30, but no-one was around. I decided to go back home and grab a book."

"I can't believe how many times you've read that book and you're still not tired of it! My mom used to read me that book all the time, and when I was 10 by the time she said "Once upon a time," I had had it!"

I laughed sarcastically. "Jerome you should appreciate books and their content. This is the only book available in the City. Even if you've read something a thousand times, in the end you can always learn something new about it."

"Sorry Miss Sensitive…"

I kicked his foot.

"Ouch!"

"That was for insulting the most sensitive of them all!"

"Ha, ha Perrie, You're so funny." He said.

Jerome and I don't talk to each other much for a reason. His comments set me on edge. I walked further to the corner of the Square and spotted my favorite tree. I ran to it and quickly took my seat. I love this tree for one reason, and one reason only. I actually don't sit at the base. When no one is looking, I climb to the top and perch in the branches. Nobody can spot me there, and I have peace and quiet. (Aside from the fact I am in the center of a city.) I looked to my left, then to my right. No-one was looking. I quickly slipped to the backside of the tree and started to climb. I grabbed the first branch, then the second, and hoisted myself up. Once I got to the top of the tree, I perched on the 35th branch. Up here it's peaceful and secluded. I feel like I'm on top of the world! I looked around below me. I saw Jerome sell his least favorite cow, Bessie, to Mr. Cane. Mr. Cane was a tall, thin man. Nobody knew much about him…he stayed away from everyone and everything. Mr. Cane took Bessie over to a pasture. I wonder what he was doing…..Wait a second, he just…he let her go! Nobody lets food go free! I tried to yell to Jerome.

"Jerome!" I shouted. "JEROME!!"

He looked around but I don't think he could see me. I was about to scream at him again, but I knew it was going to be a waste of effort. I felt guilty watching Bessie wander around in the fields next to the Square, so I decided to retrieve her and bring her back to Jerome. I mean if Mr. Cane wasn't going to take care of her, she should be returned to her rightful owner. I looked around to make sure nobody was watching, and climbed down the tree. When I got to the base, I ran behind the lamps hoping no-one would see me. I quickly slipped through the East gate and was standing in the fields. The fields seemed to go on forever, with their majestic rolling hills and distinguished color span. I saw Bessie munching on the soybeans over to my left.

"Bessie, come here girl, nice cow." I said, calmly.

"Moo." She responded.

She leisurely trotted towards me. She is such a little dumb-dumb. I grabbed her leash and snuck her back into the Square.

"Let's get you back to your owner, shall we?" I said to myself.

I looked around and spotted Jerome's stand, but he wasn't there. I took Bessie to her stable, and wrapped her leash around the post.

"Stay here and be a good cow, okay?" I said quietly, petting her head.

I ran back to my tree and climbed up as quickly as I could, hoping no-one would notice.

"31, 32, 33, 34, 35!" I said to myself.

I lifted myself to the 35th branch (as usual) and looked at the damage I left behind me. People didn't notice my commute to the tree, but they noticed Bessie was back.

"Hey, didn't Jerome sell Bessie to Mr. Cane 10 minutes ago?" Said someone.

"I thought so…." said another.

Everyone started to murmur about Bessie's return, but after about 5 minutes they shrugged it off. Jerome returned to his stand and saw Bessie.

"I thought I sold you….Hm. I must be losing it." He said.

Thankfully, that was over. Some crazy things happen in the Square every day.

CHAPTER 2: NIGHTMARE ON SHIMMER STREET

It was getting dark outside, and the lights in the Square came on. I didn't get to read much today, considering what happened earlier, so I decided to go home. I climbed down the tree and went to the West end of the Square, strolling down Sheer Road and onto Shimmer Street; where I live. In the square, there are 4 gates. They follow a compass, being North, South, East, and West. The North gate is where they put people to rest. The only other reason a person would go there is because they committed a serious crime and are given a trial at court. The trials are almost never won. The Judge isn't very kind and doesn't show very much mercy.

At the West and South gates are the housing areas. The housing areas are only big enough for the amount of people in the city. No more, no less. That is, unless you go missing. In the Pure City we aren't allowed to reproduce. If someone goes missing, one lucky couple will be told by the Officials to have a child. If they refuse they will be given a penalty of committing an offense. If you ask me, I think it's kind of harsh. I must be happy though, and I can't say anything about it.

The Eastern gate is where the fields are. The fields are where the farmers grow the food for the citizens of the city. There is only a limited amount of people who get to be farmers though. They are chosen from birth. Some people say it is an honor to become a farmer, while others call it a punishment. I personally think it is an honor, because you were special to someone; they made you a farmer! It's a rare thing to do! I don't understand why people don't like it…

I was getting extremely tired all of the sudden. I ran to my house on Shimmer Street and hit my head on a lamppost.

"OUCH!" I said, rubbing my sore forehead.

After I regained my senses, I went inside and ran to my bathroom. There was my mirror, waiting for me.

"Awake…" I mumbled.

"How may I be of service to you, Perrie Fawn?" She said.

"Check my spark's power."

"Power at 20%. It's time for you to return your spark to the Officials, Perrie."

That's funny; she never was so firm before. I guess robots have mood swings too.

"Alright…calm down, I'm going." I said. "Authorize opening of heart gate."

"Authorized."

There was that buzzing in my chest again.

"Spark removed. Would you like me to send spark to the Officials?" She said.

"Please." I said, getting really sleepy.

"Sending spark. Spark sent. Have a nice night, Ms. Fawn."

"Thanks."

She powered down and went to sleep. That didn't sound like such a bad idea to me either. I slipped on my pajama dress and sunk under the covers of my sleeping tube. The sleeping tubes looked like pipes cut in half; once you got under the covers a glass covering would rise over you. I fell asleep quickly, being tired from running around all day.

The same woman from the other night's dream took my hand and started to sing. I was wailing and crying, but she was all I had at the moment. Her voice was soft. It cracked a little, but it was ok. She started to cradle me in her arms. I was clutching her shoulder. She lovingly looked at me and started to cry too.

"Where did he go …?" I said.

"He went away and won't be coming back. I will be here for you through the hard times we are going through. I love you very much. I loved him very much." She said wiping the tears off my cheeks.

"Then why didn't you go after him!?" I asked trying to hide a sniffle.

"I…I……" She started to tear up again.

"You'll understand when you're older." She said.

"Did he hire a babysitter?" I said.

"What?"

"Since he's gone, didn't he hire a babysitter to care for us while he's away?"

She started to cry, but she smiled.

"Yes. He hired Michael to take care of us while he is away."

I didn't know who she was talking about. A man walked into the room.

"I heard my name!" He smiled and ruffled my hair.

"Mikey!" I said beaming with excitement.

I had no control over what I was saying or doing. I really hate dreams sometimes. I heard a boom in the distance. The excitement quickly drained from

Michael's face. The woman told me to be quiet. Her face was flushed white.

"What is it?" I said.

I woke up gasping for air. I looked at the clock. It was 4:28 in the morning. I don't understand why I am having all these nightmares! I have been eating healthy, I've been doing what I am supposed to, and I'm at peace. The Officials say that as long as you don't disobey them and do what you are supposed to, you will never be afraid, unhealthy, or be disturbed in any way! Maybe I should stop reading the fairytale about the girl who gets lost in the woods on her way to a relative's house. It gives me chills every time, but it feels good. These chills I get from the nightmares are obviously not good. Maybe I should go see the doctor tomorrow.

CHAPTER 3: A VISIT TO THE DOCTOR

I decided to go through with my idea that I got in the wee hours of the morning, and go to the doctor. I know that these dreams probably mean nothing, but I like to be sure of my state of health. I mean, we are supposed to be happy in The Pure City, and these dreams are a little unsettling. I went to my front doorstep and saw my package. Inside it was my spark. I went to the bathroom again, and turned to step in front of the mirror.

"Good morning, Perrie." She said in her mechanical voice.

"Hello. I just need authorization for the Spark today." I said.

"Of course; authorizations processing...processing.. authorizations complete."

"Thank you."

"I hope you enjoy your traits today, Ms. Fawn. Give greetings to the Doctor."

How did she know about that I wondered? "I will. Good day..." I said.

"Is there anything else I can do for you?"

"Actually, you can power down for the day."

"I'm sorry Ms. Fawn; I could not interpret what you just requested. Please ask again?

"Please power down for the day. I don't appreciate you listening in to my conversations…with myself…"

She made a strange creaking and scraping noise. "OUCH!" I said. It was hurting my ears.

"I'm sorry Miss Fawn, forgive me, powering down." She said, and then the mirror went black.

That was a little strange. I've never heard her make that noise before….I'm sure she was just having some technical difficulties. Another reason I'm not especially fond of robots.

I got up and got dressed in my same outfit I had the day before.

"I should probably wash this………" I said, lazily. "I'll wash them when they get dirty!"

I think I have the lazy trait today. I suddenly didn't feel motivated to do anything but watch the T.V. all day long…and eat fried chessomacs. Chessomacs were a mix of cheese and bread. A long time ago they used to be called "curds" but now we call them chessomacs. They taste great when they're fried.

I went outside and the air smelled like fruit tarts. I haven't tried one, but I've heard they are sublime! I put my hand into my pockets and felt for wires. My pockets were completely empty! I guess I'm broke….no matter though, the Doctor will still see me. Everyone in The Pure City needs to be pure in health, so I'm sure the Officials will let me have an appointment. Wires are what we use to pay people with in The Pure City. We can also trade each other, but nobody really likes that anymore. I'm not sure why. Five wires give the value of one book. One wire is very great in value, and can get you a long way. I had one a few weeks ago, but I guess I spent it all….

I need a job. That will come to me when I most need it though. The Officials can help me choose the best career path for my traits I receive the most. It's been a rumor that if the traits you get are the same for a while, those are your true traits. Those are the traits you were meant to have. It's really rare when that happens though. I looked at the time.

"8:58 a.m." I said. "The Doctor usually opens up his office around 9:30. I should probably be on my way. His office is in the southern gate."

The office was in the very back of the southern gates. Far beyond the mansions and the small houses was the Doctor's office. The office was a small place, and not many people went there. Everyone in The Pure City was in pretty good shape. The poor old Doctor has been here since the beginnings of The Pure City. I'm not even sure how old he is! He is a stout, strong little man. He is very tough and has survived a lot of hardships. Personally, I look up to him a little. Even though he could possibly be losing it being all alone out in the middle of the southern gate, he has pulled through. I enjoy being alone too. I've learned that if you get too attached to some things, it can be used against you in any way possible. That is why I'm the quiet and shy girl who doesn't talk much, has no friends, and seems to be invisible. I'm just fine with that!

I left the house at 9:43 a.m. I walked leisurely down Sheer Rd. and took the left at the curb. When I got to the Square, everyone was going about their usual business, selling, buying, admiring, and just being happy. I heard someone whisper something to a news boy, and all of the sudden his eyes opened wide and his mouth dropped open. I swear I could have thrown an apple in his mouth and it would have gone down his throat; his mouth was so big! He started to run around and whisper to people. Everyone started to gasp, and one girl started to cry. He finally came to me.

"What's happening?" I said.

He started to whisper, saying, "Casey Simons has disappeared."

"Who's Casey Simons?" I asked.

"No time for questions, I'm just here to deliver the news!" He said, and scuttled off.

I did wonder who Casey Simons was, but I didn't have the energy or curiosity to inquire further about the poor girl. Is this what it's like to be lazy? I really don't like it at all! I feel like I constantly don't want to do anything and if I do my mind will whine and complain about it! Thank goodness these traits are temporary. I continued to the southern gate of the Square. I looked around and quickly slipped through the gate. I looked down the vast span of concrete mixed with crystals that was before me. The houses looked so elegant. They matched the small white crystal reflection given off by the road. Most of the houses were gray with small white porches on each one. They looked a little identical, but it was harmonious with the monotonous feel of the city in general. Most people get tired of the repetitive nature of the houses and the buildings, but I think it adds a certain grace to it. I slowly walked down the pavement. After a few minutes I had to cross a river. The Pure City is surrounded by one river, almost like a moat. The river is just to separate some houses from the others. The mansions are on the other side of the river. They are only meant for the people who were the first to be in The Pure City. The only bad thing about the river is that there aren't any bridges. The river was meant to separate the amazing from the peasants, after all. The Doctor was one of the first to come to the city, so I had to get over the river. The question is, how? I looked around for something I could use as an overpass, but I had no luck. I stuck my hand in the water and let it go loose. The current wasn't too horrible. I put my right foot in and stood there for a second. I didn't float away. I would dry off by the time I reached the Doctor's office. I put both my feet in. I stuck my hand underwater to feel for a stick. I found one!

"I'll use this to test how deep it is in front of me." I said to myself.

I poked the stick in front of me and felt muddy ground. I really had to hold on to it so as to not let the current sweep it away! I slowly took a few steps forward, so far so good. I repeated these steps a few times more, and I was close to the middle of the river. I pushed the stick in front of me and felt the ground. It must have been getting harder, considering there would be sand in the middle of a river. I took a step forward, and was underwater. Looking back, I saw the stick lodged underneath a large rock. I was quickly swept down the river. I was caught off guard and was holding water in my mouth. I couldn't swim upwards, the current was too strong. It looks completely fine from the top of the river, but underneath, it's a nightmare in the form of liquid. I tried to swim against the current, but there was no point. I soon lost all the oxygen I was holding in, and everything went black.

CHAPTER 4: HANNAH

When I woke up I started to cough up water. I felt like it was stuck in my lungs and I was gasping for air. My stomach was aching, my head hurt, and I had no idea where I was. I coughed up some more water and looked around. I was in a field and it was foggy. I looked to my right and there was just some grass and the river again. It was the same on my left. In front of me was a small patch of dirt. I felt small sprinkles of rain drip onto my hair. That's just great, I'm super wet and it's going to rain soon. I stood up and stepping into the patch of dirt. I narrowed my eyes and looked around but I couldn't see much of anything. I went to my left and saw a silhouette of a tree. As the sprinkles were turning into small drops of rain, I ran for the tree. I stopped abruptly, as the tree started to move. Then I saw….two…trees…I saw the second tree drop to the ground. Then I heard a scream. Those obviously weren't trees.

"IS ANYONE OUT THERE? ARE YOU HURT?" I yelled.

I saw the first person start to walk towards me. The silhouette formed the shape of a man. I started to run into the fog, still not entirely sure what my plan was. I looked back and saw nothing but the fog again. I heard quiet footsteps going to my right. I got down on my hands and knees and crawled to the left. I was playing a game of cat and mouse with a possible hostile or a possible savior. I didn't know which this person was, but I wasn't going to take my chances. After all, the second person screamed for a reason. I wonder where they ran off to. At the moment, I shouldn't be concerned with the other person, because now I see the first person running towards me! I ran in the opposite direction, but he was slowing down. He started to limp almost...

"Help, please…" He said.

He sure didn't sound like a man! The voice he had shared a small hint of femininity to it. It was a low voice, but it had a high-pitched edge on the end. As he limped closer, I saw it was not a man; in fact, it was a woman!

"Please, don't go! I'm not going to hurt…you..." She said. She then decided to fall at my feet.

I didn't know who this woman was! I felt bad, leaving her there. It's starting to rain and I need to find some form of shelter! She was probably dead anyway. I looked back and saw a faint outline of her fallen body. I couldn't just leave her there to sink into the muddy ground. I felt too guilty. I ran back to the outline and heard her groan in pain. I tried to pick her up, but she was too heavy. I decided to wait there for a few minutes, just telling her everything was going to be okay. The sprinkles were now turning into a consistent and light rain. We needed to get to shelter.

"Be right back." I told her.

"Ungh." She said, slowly nodding her head and trying to regain her senses.

I needed a way to mark my path so I wouldn't get lost in the fog. I found a small rock in the dirt patch and started to draw a line from the dirt patch through the muddy grass. I looked for an outline of a branch or any type of large rock, but had no luck. Finally I came across a log by a river. I wasn't sure if it was the same river as the city's or not, but it was something to keep me dry. I ran back along my line I created and put both my arms underneath the girl's. I used all my strength to pull her.

"On three, I'm going to pull you backwards. Okay? If you could try to help push, that would be splendid." I told her.

She used all her strength, grimacing in pain, and walked backwards as I pulled her. We gradually made our way towards the log. It started to pour just as we were at the river. I stuffed her into the log, and I went to the opposite end. She was crying out for a doctor.

"I need a covering. I've been shot in my left foot..." She said, caterwauling.

"Of course you do, I'll go and find something." I replied.

"You can't. Its pouring rain and you're already too wet." She said.

"I'm trying to save your life!!" I said. I mean, if she didn't want my help, so be it!

"I understand, and I am very grateful for that. Regrettably, I was the one that placed myself into this situation, and I deserve what I got. You need to save yourself, get back to the city." She said. She then opened up a small compact mirror and said, "Authorize emergency transfer."

"Authorized." It replied.

"Wait! I don't even know who you are!!" I said.

"My name is Hannah, and you're going to be alright. I see good in you." She said.

Only after it happened did I realize what she was doing. My chest started buzzing.

"Wait, you can't just…!" I said, desperately trying to convince her to stop. She couldn't stop it though, it was already done.

A spark floated out of her chest, and flew into mine. My eyes teared up over this girl I barely knew; she never even asked my name, and sacrificed her life for me! I started to sniffle. I was cold, alone, wet, and I just met a girl who died for me. I almost wanted to tear the spark out of me and die with her. I felt so guilty. I sat in the log for what seemed to be forever, and the rain let up enough for me to step outside without being immediately soaked. I was dry and it was just sprinkling now. The fog wasn't as thick as it was when I met Hannah, and that was good. What was bad, was the fact that I just let a girl die for me and didn't give her my extra spark so she could continue living. I will never forget Hannah. I wonder what happened to that first person who was following me. I already knew what had happened, but I try not to think about it. Everyone returned their sparks to the Officials by now because it was getting into the evening. His spark ran out before he could ever get help. I shouldn't say that, maybe he found a way out of the fog! Maybe he was sitting at home with his family and friends, snuggled close to a fire and talking about his adventure. I knew though, deep in my heart, that he was dead and alone. He was the same as Hannah.

I decided to go back into the log and take Hannah's compact mirror. I didn't even know these were out yet! I felt horrible having to pick-pocket the girl who saved my life, but I knew she would have wanted me to have it. I took out the mirror and went outside.

"Mirror, I'm lost. Where am I?" I asked it.

"You are in the Western province." She said.

"How far away am I from The Pure City?"

"You are exactly 134 miles from the destined location."

On foot it would take around 5 days to get back. I didn't have a spark that would last that long. Surely Hannah connected this mirror to her home mirror. Maybe I can ask how far away her home is! A person wouldn't take a 5 day trip to hurt her! Would they..?

"Mirror, how far away is my home?" I asked.

"Home is about 5 miles away." She said.

5 miles would only take me about an hour and a 20 minutes!

"Calculate route to home, avoid rivers if possible." I told her.

"Calculating, alright, here is your map to follow." She said. The mirror displayed an image of where I was, and started to show a route. If I'm going to keep moderately dry, I should hurry. I started in a jog, and then gradually went into a run.

CHAPTER 5: HANNAH'S HOME

It didn't take as long as I thought it would; since I started to run. The path I took involved crossing through a lot of dirt and grass patches. Eventually, I came to a small dirt road. The road wasn't very long, and at the end I saw a few small shacks. I ran as fast as I ever could. When I reached the shacks, I saw it built up to a petite town in the middle of nowhere! I thought that all these smaller towns didn't exist anymore. I went to the center of town. I looked around and saw an elderly woman sitting in a rocking chair.

"Excuse me, can you tell me where I am?" I asked.

"A dungeon" She said, looking at me suspiciously.

"What do you mean a dungeon?" I said, perplexed. There was no need for dungeons because there were no criminals!

"A place only for the wicked." She said, still looking at me funny. "Go back to where you came from."

"Well that's the thing, you see, I don't know where I am.

"Then figure it out!" She said, and wobbled on inside her shack.

I am so confused.

"MA'AM?! WAIT! HAVE YOU HEARD OF A HANNAH? IS ANYONE'S NAME HANNAH IN THIS PLACE?" I yelled.

She cracked the door open just a bit.

"What do you want with Hannah?" She said.

"I would like to know where she lives. I am her friend, and she invited me to her house." I am such a bad liar…

"She lives next door. Now, go away!" She said, and slammed the door.

What a rude woman! Everyone in The Pure City is happy! I've never seen anyone that grumpy. I went the house over, and opened up the compact.

"Mirror can you open the door for me? I left my keys inside the house." I lied.

"Of course, Hannah." She replied.

The door on Hannah's house crumbled and I stepped inside. A woman was waiting for me. She was the same woman I have been having dreams about. Then my little sister, Stacy, came out of nowhere!

"Stacy?! What are you doing here?! YOU'RE DEAD!!!" I screamed.

I woke up in a bed. My heart was beating faster than it ever had, and I was sweating. On the side of my bed was a man in a long white coat. Standing beside him was a short young girl, wearing a long brown dress. She had the body of a 12 year old, with the feet of a man. I looked down at myself; I was wearing a hospital gown. I coughed up a bucket load of water.

"Go and another bucket." said the man in the long white coat.

"Yes Papa." She said.

She came back with a bucket and told me to cough the water into it. I did as she said. After I was done, I had some questions to ask this man.

"Where am I?" I said, slightly frustrated.

"You're at the Doctor's office." Said the man.

"Where is the Doctor?" I said.

"You obviously don't get around much, do you? I'm Doctor Maxwell." He said.

"How did I get here, Doctor Maxwell?" I asked, still slightly frazzled with reality and the dream world.

"You washed up on the shores of the North gate and the Officials found you. They used their mirrors to identify you and saw you were a citizen. They brought you here, seeing you were in a poor state of health." He said.

"How am I doing?" I asked.

"I think you can figure that one out for yourself." He said.

I could move all my fingers and toes. Thankfully, nothing was broken. I decided to get up, and that was a bad idea. I immediately started to cough up more water, but this time I coughed up small rocks and some sand. The girl caught most of it in the bucket, but there was a lot of sand they would have to clean up. I felt like my chest was weighing me down; it was probably the sand I accidentally swallowed. I felt really weak. I felt vulnerable for once in my life.

"Whoa, Perrie, you need to rest. You've been through a traumatizing experience and you're still getting a grip on your stomach. You'll be coughing up water and a little bit of sand most of the day. I would recommend staying in bed with the bucket." He said.

I didn't feel like I had been through anything traumatizing. I think the dream was more dramatic and scary than the river. Just to make Doc. Maxwell be quiet, I went back to the bed and pulled the covers over my head. I quickly fell asleep. I didn't dream about anything. Well, we all have dreams, but I just couldn't remember mine. When I woke up I coughed up some more rocks. I wonder how many times I hit the bottom of that river to still have this much stuff in lodged in my lungs!

"Okay, you should have most of the sand and rocks out of your lungs and whatever is left is in the stomach. You should be fit to go home tomorrow. I'm going to keep you overnight just to be sure…" Doctor Maxwell said.

Be sure of what?" I said.

"Nothing you need to be concerned about, just protocol." He said.

I got up and walked to the window. I looked outside and saw the red and orange sky as the sun set. I heard footsteps behind me and I turned around. I saw the girl who was helping Maxwell earlier. She looked up at me, and then quickly ran back to a corner.

"Hey, where are you going? What's wrong?" I said.

"I'm sorry. I was bothering you." She said quietly.

"You weren't disturbing me, you're fine." I said.

"Okay..." She said, quickly slipping back to the window. "Papa never lets me outside. If he saw me looking out the window, he would throw a fit."

"I'm not going to get you in trouble am I?" I said.

"No, no it's worth it. I have always wanted to see the sunset."

I looked around hoping Maxwell wasn't anywhere close. I would feel bad if I got this girl in trouble.

"Why doesn't your father let you outside?" I asked.

"He said it is a dangerous world out there. I think he just fears of me being taken away." She replied.

"You're talking about the disappearances, aren't you?"

"Yes. He fears them. Do not ask me why, I only know he is trying to protect me."

"Do you think your father could possibly know more about the disappearances?"

The sun finally set and the stars were coming out.

"He has lived longer than I have, so he may." She said. "But I must get back to work as I would not want to get in trouble. It was nice to meet you, Perrie Fawn."

"It was nice to make your acquaintance as well." I said. I never got her name.

I decided to go search for the Doctor, hoping to find some more answers about these disappearances. The Doctor's office was like one big square room with two side rooms. I was in the big square room, and obviously, the Doctor was not here. I decided to check the first side room. I walked over to the door, and it was locked. I decided I'd come back to this later. I went over to the other side of the room, to the second side room. The door wasn't locked and it opened with ease. I soon found out this was some sort of office, judging by the desk and pieces of paper scattered everywhere. Most likely it was Maxwell's office. There were file cabinets to the right with stickers attached to them. The first cabinet said: "PATIENT FILES". The second cabinet said: "VARIOUS PROJECTS THAT NEED TO BE FINISHED" Hm...Looks like the Doctor could be a procrastinator. The last file cabinet said: "JUNK". I decided to go and look in patient files. I looked under the F's and found my name, Fawn! There were 2 files. One of them was my name and the other….the other was Stacy Fawn. Why would the Doctor have a file on my little sister..? I was going to hold on to it to examine later. I walked over to the desk and looked at the papers scattered everywhere.

"Bills, letters to patients, wait…what's this? Is this a letter from the Officials?" I said.

It read:

Dear Timothy Maxwell,

We regret to inform you that your daughter has committed an offense. The offense will cost her 34 days off her light card. If you do not comply with the standard rules of receiving discipline, you will be punished severely.

Sincerely,
The Officials

I wonder what his daughter did. She seemed so sweet and quiet. Everyone is different on the inside, I guess… Wait a second; Maxwell wouldn't let her go outside… I wonder if this is the reason… I decided to keep looking around for more letters like this, but I couldn't find any. The date on the letter was about a week ago.

It was getting late and I knew that Maxwell would come to check on me and make sure I was in bed, so I decided to grab the file, the letter, and a paperclip. I ran back to bed and stuffed the file and letter underneath my pillow. I balled my fist around the paperclip as I pretended to sleep. I heard some footsteps creak up near the bed. They were heavy footsteps and I knew they were the Doctor's. Or, so I thought. I felt a cloth go around my mouth. I tried to bite the fingers holding it, but I was asleep before I knew it.

CHAPTER 6: FORGETTING

 When I woke up, I was in my bed at home. The last thing I remember was going to bed at the Doctor's office. I guess he thought I was well enough to leave. There was something poking at my hand. It was holding tight to something small, but pointy. I unrolled my fist and saw a paperclip. I must have gotten bored while in bed all day. I went to my mirror and looked at myself. I had bedhead hair, and my eyes looked ice blue. I needed to get my spark for the day. I got into a different outfit today. I wore a leather jacket with a green short sleeve shirt. The shirt had a small lacy collar on it. I then grabbed a pair of dark brown cargo pants, and got dressed. I needed to get my spark before I ran out of energy.

"Awake. I need my spark." I said in a hurry.

"Ms. Fawn, your spark has been recharged already." She replied.

"What do you mean recharged?"

"It had been *recharged* and replaced with a new one."

"Check last time spark was given to the Officials."

"Last time spark was recharged: 12:03 a.m. last night."

"I didn't send it to the Officials though."

"You forgot to and the Officials did it for you while you were sleeping."

"Okay....Well that's it for today. You deserve a day off, I insist you power down." I said.

"Okay, thank you Perrie." She said, and the mirror went black.

The Officials never do THAT much for you... I guess I must be special! It didn't seem right, but who am I to complain! I stepped outside. It was a sunny day, with no clouds in sight. I stopped for a moment and let the light sink into my face. It felt almost as good as having a spark inside you. I felt that one of my traits was carefree. I felt like I had no worries today! Everything was sunny and happy. I ran as fast as I could to the square. Everyone was here today, going about their usual business. It was a good day! I saw the book keeper, Mara. I felt for some wires in my pocket and I pulled out 3 of them. I didn't work or anything, so how could I have gotten these? Who cares?! I feel rich!

"Mara, Mara!" I yelled, excitedly.

"Ah, Perrie, I thought I would see you today." She said.

"Mara!" I said as I hugged her. She was almost like a mother to me. "I've missed you and your books!"

"Well, you're in luck. I have a new book with me today." She said.

"A NEW BOOK?!" I said, squeaking like a child.

"Shhh…Yes, I have a new book. I wrote it myself. It's a special gift for my best customer." She whispered.

"What is it called? What's it about?!" I whispered, still filled with excitement.

"I'll let you name it. It's about a girl who lives in the city. It is a true story." She whispered. "Now take it and run along! You have some reading to do."

I did as she told me, without hesitation. I ran to my favorite tree, looked around, and climbed up with the book on my head. It was a difficult task to do, considering I was trying to balance a book on my head, with no hands to help, at an angle that was not meant for balancing things. Thankfully, just before it fell off my head, I got to the 35th branch and caught it. I took off my leather jacket and set it on top of the branch, considering I would be here for a while and needed a comfy perch. What I love about this tree is that on the 35th branch you can lean backwards and the branches almost form a chair for you to sit in. It's great for reading and observing. I started to dive into the book.

"Perrie, I need your help. I know what happened to Casey Simons. I was there. We need to talk. There is more going on than you would think.

THE END"

The book had many more pages, but they were all empty. Mara was crying out for help. We needed to speak where no one could hear. I pondered where that could be.

"I know! The East-Gate's fields!" I said to myself.

The fields were a quiet place and hardly anyone came through. Surely we could talk there in secret. I peeked over the top of the branches and looked around. I waited for everyone to go back to their homes and eat lunch. I was getting hungry myself, but at the moment I had more important things to do. I grabbed my jacket and jumped from the top of the tree. Right before I hit the ground I rolled. It was still painful, but rolling helps. The tree wasn't a SUPER huge tree anyway. I needed to get to Mara before she closed up shop.

"Mara!" I yelled.

"Oh Perrie! What is it dear?" She said.

"I loved your book. Here, you can have it back. I want you to keep your own work." I said, handing her the book. "Maybe I can help you finish it? I noticed it was cut off, just a little, and I think I have some marvelous ideas for it! Why don't you meet me in the East Gate's Fields tomorrow at noon?" I said.

"That sounds great, Ms. Fawn." She said, faking a smile.

"Alright, see you tomorrow!" I said, and ran off to my tree.

I ran behind the tree and started climbing. I got to the 35th branch and sighed. I almost felt as if I had forgotten something. I reclined into the branches that shaped a chair and looked at the sky. It was too bright though, so I turned on my side and looked through the leaves. I saw Jerome selling jam. I saw a florist selling bouquets of flowers to a gentleman. The man was dressed in a black suit, bow tie, and top hat. It almost looked as if he was off to get married. Since the florist' cart was right below the tree, I decided to listen in on their conversation.

"That will be 1 wire please." She said.

"Of course." He said, handing her the wire. He fiddled around for it in his pocket for a while, and almost pulled out 4! He must be rich.

"Is it a special day?" The florist said.

"Yes. Today is the day I will ask a special woman in my life to spend the rest of her days with me." He said with a beaming smile.

"I'm so happy for you! I hope she says yes." She said.

"I hope so too." He said, slightly laughing, but then he stopped smiling. He trotted off quickly.

I wonder what upset him. Maybe he wasn't kidding around when he said he hopes she says yes? There is another reason love is not a good idea. You're always at risk of losing your lover. One day they love you, the next day they found someone else, or you're not good enough for them anymore. I will never get into a relationship anyway; I've seen too much pain and suffering.

I rolled over on my other side to look through the leaves, but all I saw was the wall that covers the square. I reached out to touch it. It felt like wood and concrete all in one. It was an interesting texture. After a while I felt a small shock of electricity go through my finger.

"Ouch!" I said, and started sucking my sore finger. It was probably the Officials. They don't like you messing with all the important stuff. In my opinion, the Officials don't like you to have a lot of fun. It was getting into the afternoon and I was bored. I decided to just go home and re-read my only book. Climbing down the tree, I stopped. I saw Mara talking to an Official. I decided to stay back for just a second. I saw her point to my tree. Then the Official started to walk towards my tree. I started to panic, wondering if I should run, or stay.

The Official walked up to me.

"Ms. Fawn?" He said.

"Yes? How may I help you officer?" I said.

"I just need your input on a few things." He said.

I've never heard of Officials conducting surveys before...

"Okay I just need a simple yes or no for 3 questions. Question 1: Have you had any friends or family that have been taken away or have been part of the "disappearances" lately?" He asked.

"No." I said.

"Okay, question 2: Have you obtained any information about the disappearances from anyone? Even if they're rumors, have you heard anything?" He asked.

I was listening, but something was happening behind him. There were more Officials. They were all gathered around the news boy. I saw him mouth "NO!" Then, they grabbed both of his arms, and took him away!

"Hey! Where are they taking him?" I asked the Official.

"Who?" He asked looking around. He saw the news boy. "Looks like he has committed an offense. That is Official business, AND you didn't answer my question." He asked?

"Concerning your question; no. What has he done?" I asked.

"He hasn't done anything; you shouldn't be concerned. We are trying to obtain as much information about these disappearances as possible. We are just as confused as the rest of the city is about it." He said.

"Last question: Do you have any idea who may be behind these disappearances?" He asked.

"I don't know. None of us know. They just happen." I said.

"Alright, thank you for your cooperation. As a reward, we will let you choose your traits for tomorrow." He said holding out a list.

The list read:

Aggressiveness

Agreeableness

Assertiveness

Compliance

Courage

Creativity

Curiosity

Dishonesty

Excited

Extraversion

Femininity

Honesty

Humility

Introversion

Irritability

Liberalism

Likability

Loyalty

Modesty

Nurturance

Obedience

Self-control

Tender-mindedness

Timidity

Tolerance

"You may choose 8." said the Official.

"I choose…… loyalty, modesty, courage, introversion, creativity, curiosity, likability, and self-control." I said.

He pressed a few buttons on the list, and said "Have a good day, Ms. Fawn."

I guess I was wrong. I thought the Officials knew more about these disappearances than we do. We are all in the dark on this one.

I went back to my house and decided to go to bed. I went into the bathroom to send my spark back to the Officials.

"Thank you Ms. Fawn. I hope you have good dreams tonight." She said, after it was over.

I wonder if I will dream about anything tonight. I climbed under the covers of my sleep tube. I still can't remember what I dreamt about last night. All I can remember is a hand, and falling asleep…I think…or at least that's what I thought. It's still a little fuzzy. The glass went over my head and I got really sleepy. Before I knew it, I was fast asleep, once again.

CHAPTER 7: ROBBED

When I woke up I hit my head on the glass.

"What the heck! Why didn't you move?" I yelled to the lifeless covering over my head.

I tried to get out, but it wouldn't budge. I heard some commotion on my T.V. downstairs. I heard some of my neighbors yelling at each other.

"Open." I said to the glass.

Nothing happened.

"OPEN!" I yelled.

Still, nothing was responding. I felt trapped in this small space.

"Calm down Perrie; this could be a good thing. After all, people are stupid." I said.

I laid there for a few minutes, trying to contemplate what I should do. I got an idea. I was going to use that paperclip I had a few days ago to try and mess up the cables. Hopefully I left it in the bed. I rummaged around through the sheets, and found it! It was lodged between the mattress and the sides of the tube. I bent it into an s shape and looked for the control panel. I found a few small screws. I moved my pillow over and tried to unscrew the screws with my nails. Slowly, one by one, I got all 4 of them out. I opened the small panel and inside I saw 3 wires. One was blue, the other was yellow, and the last was green.

I remember in school, when we were learning about sleeping tubes, one of them is light. I can't remember the others! I haven't been in school for 5 years now. We only have 4 grades. We start when we are 1 and we go until we are 12. Each year lasts 3 years. In the 1st year, we learn about talking and how to act. In the 2nd year, we start to learn about the many things the city has to offer, (one of those things being sleeping tubes.) In the 3rd year, we learn about jobs we do when we are older. In the last year, we do a lot of tests, reviewing what we have learned. If we pass those tests, we get a certificate that lets us work. We can all start work when we are 16. It is not required, but it is recommended. I was too busy taking care of Stella to work. She died only a year ago.

I was trying to figure out which wire was which. I was guessing that the yellow wire was for light. I took a chance and cut the green wire.

"Terminating oxygen." A robotic voice coming from the tube said.

THAT IS NOT GOOD. I quickly cut the blue wire and the glass covering the tube opened. I got out and closed it again. I can't risk it possibly sucking out the oxygen in my house. When I got a hold of my nerves, I looked around. What I saw made my jaw drop. All of my things were pulled out of my drawers and on the floor. The overhead light was broken and sparking with electricity. I ran downstairs and my predictions were right. My fridge was open and empty. My stove was turned on and it was opened. Thankfully, this didn't happen a long time ago, otherwise my house would have been on fire. I closed it and turned it off before anything else could happen. In my living room, my couch was torn to shreds. My T.V. was left alone though. I went outside and everybody else was yelling and screaming at each other.

"YOU TOOK MY FOOD! YOU DIRTY THIEF!" Said one person.

"NO I DIDN'T! I KNOW YOU TOOK MINE!" Said the other.

It was pure chaos. I ran over to a neighbor of mine. I didn't know her name; I just knew she lived next to me.

"What's going on?!" I asked.

"I asked the Officials and they said someone robbed us. They thought it was the same person who has been behind the disappearances." She said.

She was probably right.

"How did they get past our security systems though?" I asked.

"I don't know. I thought it was impossible, but apparently, it's not." She said.

She was probably right. I needed to talk to someone of high status though. I looked around and saw an Official. I needed a second opinion on what happened.

"Hey! Official!" I shouted.

"Yes, Ms……Fawn?" He replied.

"What happened here?" I asked.

"We think the person who is behind the disappearances is responsible for this."

"Has this happened to everyone?"

"So far, everyone from the East to the West gates has experienced this."

"What are you going to do about it then? Are you going to be able to do anything?"

"We are working hard to calm everyone down. There will be a special report on T.V. at 6 p.m. tonight. We noticed no one's T.V.s were taken." He said. "Everything is coming under control, but I would suggest you stay in your home for the day."

I don't understand why we have to stay in our trashed up homes. But, I decided to anyway. I went back inside and closed my door. Looking around, I sighed. I don't exactly know what I'm going to do. I went to my fridge and closed it. I hadn't noticed until now, but my table had cut marks all over it. It almost looked as if some sort of weapon had scratched it.

"Wait! I shouldn't touch anything. This is a crime scene, and everything could possibly be evidence!" I said to myself.

I needed to wait for an Official to come and check this out. I waited for what seemed an eternity, and I just couldn't wait any longer. I went back upstairs and on my bedside table was Hannah's compact mirror. I ran back downstairs and went to the table.

"Mirror, awaken." I said.

"How can I help you, Ms. Fawn?" It said.

Wait, how did I get this? I don't remember ever owning a compact mirror…. I thought about it for a few seconds.

"Oh wait! I remember!" I said. I had gotten this from the Officials. They gave it to me a long time ago. I can't exactly remember what it was for though…

"Yes, Identify." I said, showing the mirror the scratches.

"Those are scratches from a knife, Ms. Fawn." It said.

"Identify type of knife." I said.

"It is a butcher's knife." She said. "I am calculating nearest rou....457.......The Pure City started over 100 years ago....! What is it you ask?" She said.

That's weird; I've never seen a mirror glitch before.

"Off." I said.

The screen went black. Things are glitching up today. I went back to my table. I was missing a knife from my kitchen, but it wasn't as big as a butcher's knife. I had one like a butcher's knife, but it was considerably smaller. It could possibly have been my knife. I looked around, and found it lying underneath the table. Why would a thief decided to chop the table up? He/she didn't even take the knife afterwards! Maybe he/she was trying to chop something else up. I didn't pick up the knife; it had the thief's prints on it. I needed to look for more evidence, something that would give me a clue to where the thief went. My rug in the living room was crinkled up. My window in the kitchen was open, but it's not big enough for an adult to fit through. It couldn't have been a child. There are no children living in the city at the moment. I was getting off focus. The thief obviously opened that window to distract everyone from where they really escaped. I had to put myself in the thief's shoes to think about what I would do. If I was a thief, I would've gone someplace away from the window. If I was leading people off my trail with the window, I would go completely opposite of there. I looked behind me. There were trails of wreckage everywhere. I was dealing with no amateur. They knew what they were doing. The only thing that was behind me was a wall and the stairs leading to my room. There was only one other way out. I ran upstairs, and into my room. It was just as I thought; the thief had opened my window and jumped into the bushes at the back of my house. I ran back outside and went behind my house. I tried to get underneath the bushes, but it was difficult. I decided to get the hedge clippers and trimmed the bush's underbrush so I could get underneath. I was looking for something and I found it. By the way, These were no ordinary bushes. These were thistlebrush. Thistlebrush looked like normal bushes on the outside, but inside, they were full of spikes and thorns. If you would fall into one, you would fall into the middle. Thankfully, this thief didn't know about the spiky trap underneath. I carefully maneuvered my hand through the spikes and grabbed it. I pulled out the small piece of cloth that was torn off the thief's clothes. It was black and the stitching was a different style. I had never seen it before. It was almost as if someone had sewed B's into the sides. I didn't know how much this was going to help me, but I held on to it anyway.

When I went back inside, it was getting into the late afternoon. The Officials said there would be a special report about this on the T.V. at 6. I looked at the clock. It was 5:45. I had about 15 minutes to waste. I couldn't fix anything up, because everything was evidence for the Officials. For all I know, the thief could've touched everything. The more evidence, the closer we get to finding him. I decided to go back outside and sit on my front step. I didn't do much. I mostly watched a married couple fight over which one of the neighbors was the thief. I was accused multiple times just because I'm quiet and keep to myself. After a while they both agreed it was someone else and the wife started to cry about how sorry she was to yell at her husband.

"Ugh, relationships." I said.

I went back inside after about 13 minutes and sat on the floor next to my T.V. Three officials appeared before us.

"We come to you live tonight, addressing the matter that has come upon everyone. We do not know who this thief is, but we will catch him." Said the first Official.

"Or her" The second Official said.

The first gave the second a frustrated look.

"We will catch him, or her." The first said, frustrated.

"We ask all the citizens of the city to leave their homes as they are. The Officials are going to sweep through everyone's home for evidence, and they will clean it up for you. In the meantime, you are going to be provided housing by us. We have set up portable homes in the Square. Each home inhabits 15 people. Everyone will be escorted to their home after this broadcast is over. We would like you to give your attention to our main Official." The third officer said.

An Official stepped onto the screen.

"I would just like to let everyone know that you will be staying in these homes for a while. In these homes we can guarantee your safety. At your actual homes, we cannot. You can either choose to stay or to live in these homes we have provided, just for a while. The choice is yours." He said, and then stepped off the screen.

The broadcast was over.

CHAPTER 8: SHOULD I STAY OR SHOULD I GO

I wasn't sure if I should go and live in those homes or not. I was still trying to get a grasp on why this happened, how the thief got past our security systems, and who it was. Could it have been the same person behind the disappearances? Or was it someone completely different? HOW DID THEY GET PAST THE INPENETRABLE SECURITY SYSTEM?! I had so many questions on my mind; it was making my head spin. I heard a knock on the door. When I opened it, it was an Official. I was guessing he was here to escort me to the pre-built homes.

"Are you going to stay or are you going to come with me?" He said. He didn't sound very old. His voice cracked when he talked.

"Can you give me a few minutes? I'm trying to get my grip on the whole situation still. Come back tomorrow and I can give you my answer." I said, still a little confused.

"Fine, I'll come back tomorrow, but we both know you'll have to come with me in the end." He said.

"What?" I asked, but he was gone.

The Officials wouldn't force me to go, would they? They said it was your choice after all. The kid probably didn't hear his orders right. In reality, I wanted to stay home. I was going to hope the thief or the person behind the disappearances would see me as an easy target; when they would try to take me I would catch them instead. I sent my spark to the Officials. After the giant ordeal I had been through today, I thought it was best to sleep on the idea of staying home.

CHAPTER 9: HOME IS WHERE THE DEATH IS

I didn't sleep in my sleeping tube. I was too afraid of the oxygen sucking vacuum still on in there. I decided to sleep on the couch. I don't think the Officials would find anything of use to them on the couch. Besides, what thief would lie on a couch before leaving the home? I was confused, frustrated, and tired. My mind just wouldn't let me sleep though. I tried to change my position multiple times, but I just couldn't find the right spot. I got up and walked around, trying to make myself feel tired- but nothing would work. I went to my fridge, but only when I opened it did I realize I was out of food. I sighed loudly, being annoyed and tired. I watched the clock into the wee hours of the morning. Then I heard someone outside.

"Who in their right mind would still be up at this hour?" I said, hypocritically.

When I looked outside, I almost screamed too. There was a girl being held by this other person. She was screaming. The person was wearing black clothing… I couldn't tell if it was a man or a woman. Whatever it was, it had one red eye, and one yellow eye. They were both slightly glowing. That plan I had before about catching the thief; it sounded way better in my head. Then, it looked at me. I quickly closed the curtains and told my bathroom mirror to call an Official to take me to the pre-built homes in the Square.

"AWAKE, QUICKLY." I yelled at my mirror.

"Please calm down Ms. Fawn. How may I help you?" She said.

"CALL AN OFFICIAL AND MAKE IT FAST. IT IS AN URGENT MATTER THAT I BE SENT TO THE PREBUILT HOMES IN THE SQUARE." I yelled at her.

"Of course; I will call them when you've calmed down." She said.

I tried to talk calmly, hoping to fool the mirror.

"I need the Officials, it is an urgent matter." I said with a funny tone.

"Of course, I am sending for help." She said.

I heard a few footsteps outside my front door. The officials couldn't have come that quickly. I quietly ran back downstairs and looked under the door. I saw a faint red and yellow glow. My heart started to beat faster and faster. I started to hyperventilate. I suddenly remembered that I hadn't recharged my spark. If you don't recharge it, you could have some slight side effects besides just being tired. I had to hurry up and get out of here, and to the Square. I needed to get out without him/her seeing me, and the only place I could do that, was out my window in my room. I had to escape just like the thief did. I quietly ran back upstairs and grabbed the compact mirror and the book of fairytales. I knew the Officials would come here sooner or later and sift through everything, so I took the only 2 things I didn't want them to have as "evidence". I needed something like a pillow to throw out the window onto the bushes; otherwise I would end up with a lot of torn skin.

"The pillow cushions!" I whispered quietly.

I grabbed one pillow cushion and threw it down onto the bush below my bedroom window. It didn't make that much noise, thankfully. I held my book tight, and jumped onto the cushion. I wasn't so quiet this time. He/she heard me and I heard its footsteps getting closer. I ran as fast as I could down Shimmer St. When I looked behind me, all I saw was pitch black. Apparently the lights weren't on tonight. Nobody is here, so I guess the Officials think it's useless to waste power. All I saw behind me were 2 floating eyes. One was red, the other yellow. I kept running, until I couldn't see the eyes anymore. The unfortunate thing was that I couldn't see anything myself, and I had no idea where I was.

I stopped and felt around me. I couldn't see anything. It was like my childhood nightmare, the dark. If those glowing eyes were real, it might become a nightmare again. I decided to get closer to the ground. I needed to get a hold of everything. When I was ready, I got up, but that was a bad idea. I hit my head on the ceiling of something and I lost consciousness.

When I awoke, it was daylight. I looked around to make sure I wasn't dreaming. I was actually still on Shimmer St. I guess I hadn't gotten very far. The person didn't either judging by how he/she was lying right next to me. I screamed. It woke up.

"Whoa, whoa it's okay! I'm not going to hurt you." It said.

"AGH!" I said, trying to scramble away.

"Hey! Stop! I'm not going to hurt you!" He said, taking off a mask.

He was wearing a mask that had two eyes glowing different colors. He looked young. I was guessing around 19, but I don't know.

"What is that thing?" I said, pointing to the mask.

"It's a helmet that helps me see in the dark. The red eye detects life, and the yellow eye has night vision." He said.

"Who are you, and why were you gripping that girl last night?!" I asked.

"My name is Zak." He said. "That was not a girl that you were looking at."

"Who was it then?"

"I believe it was the person behind the robberies. I was trying to ask her some questions, but she threatened to scream. When I saw you, I knew you would call the Officials. I tried to knock on your door, but you were afraid. I could see you jump through your window. I tried to follow you, to calm you down, but you ran underneath this bench and conked yourself on the head. The thief had already escaped when I looked at you house, and I had nothing better to do, so I decided to watch over you. Also, your spark was lying on your front step." He said, handing me the package.

I opened my compact mirror.

"Input spark, authorize?" I said.

"Authorized." She said.

I felt the buzz in my chest, and saw the spark float into me.

"Thanks, but I don't need your help. I don't need anyone's help. I'm fine on my own." I said firmly.

"Are you sure?" He said.

"I really wouldn't trust anyone who wears THAT mask." I said, pointing to his horrifying face covering.

"I wear this so I can see at night. I'm a form of secret police. I am the only one left. All of my teammates disappeared. Ever since that happened I promised myself I would find them." He said. "I never got your name..?"

"Perrie." I said.

"Well, Ms. Perrie, even though you don't need my help I'll still keep an eye on you." He said.

"No, you won't. I'm moving, today." I said.

"Really? Where would you be going if you had someone to protect you?" He said.

"I'm going to a place that is better than protection." I lied. The Square had no better protection than anything else. I didn't believe for one second that the Officials could provide safer housing if our own homes were broken into. Every single last one of our homes had impenetrable security. I still can't get over it.

"And where is that?" He said.

"Ha! Nice try, I'm not giving my location out to a guy I just met a few minutes ago." I said.

"You'll need my help. When you do, I'm going to make you beg for it." He said, smugly, and then he walked away.

I really just dislike people. Is it really that bad? I just don't like people. How hard is it to understand? When will they learn to leave me be…

I went back to my house and started to pack my things. If I was really going to go through with this, I was going to need a few things. After about 20 minutes I was finished gathering my essentials. I shoved my compact mirror into a hidden pocket in my suitcase, and stuck the fairytale book in there as well. When I stepped out of the door there was a piece of paper on my front porch with something written on it.

Underneath, Underneath

Where the sun doesn't glow,

The only light is of red

And one of yellow,

The worst nightmare of darkness

Lies in the blackness below.

Underneath, Underneath

Soon you will go.

"What?" I said, reaching down to pick up the paper.

When I had it in my hands, I blinked, and it was gone. I wasn't dreaming or anything was I? I went back into the house to look at the clock. I heard from Jerome that a trick to check if you're dreaming or not is to look at a clock once, look away, and look at it again. It said 7:00 P.M. I looked away, and then looked at it again, and nothing had changed. I wasn't dreaming. I know for a fact that I've been under stress, and it is possible to hallucinate…I shrugged it off my shoulders and grabbed my suitcase to head for the square. As I walked down the street, I looked at everyone's houses. They looked desolate, almost like a ghost town. I saw a few things out on the lawns: chairs, tables, dressers, and everything they left behind. I kept getting this spooky feeling as I strolled down the street.

CHAPTER 10: NEW HOME

When I got to the Square, I saw the Officials waiting for me. The Square was oddly quiet. I expected everyone would be bustling about outside, still doing their usual work. Either it could have been that, or everyone is too afraid to come outside. I walked up to one of the Officials.

"Hello, last night I decided it would probably be a good idea to live in one of these houses. It seems much safer than my neighborhood." I said.

"Name" He asked?

"My name is Perrie Fawn." I said.

"Perrie Fawn..." He said as he scribbled it onto a glass clipboard. "Alright, you are going to be in house 142." He said, pointing towards the western Gate.

"Okay, thank you." I said.

There were A LOT of houses in this small square. I am still not sure how they could fit all of 15 people in one of them. I soon realized that the houses were counting down from 400. It took me quite a while to get to house 142. Finally, I saw it. It was in the architectural form of a trailer. It looked incredibly small on the outside, but once you got on the inside, it felt like a mansion. I'm still not entirely sure how it was possible, but leave it to the Officials to make something impossible, possible. There were 14 other people in the center of the room. They were sitting in a circle and playing with the rug that lay underneath them. When I closed the door, they turned around to look at me. There were 4 girls and 10 guys. It didn't exactly seem fair to have only 5 girls in all, but who was I to say that. Three of the girls had brown hair, and one had blonde. The guys were a little on the shorter side, except for one of them. He was really tall. Then again, I was very short, so maybe he was just tall to me.

"Hi." I said.

"Hey" Said the giant.

"I was assigned to this house. My name is Perrie." I said.

"Okay" Said the blonde-headed girl.

They were all so quiet. I liked that.

"Which room is mine?" I asked, looking down the hallways to my right and left.

"You can take the last one in the right hall." Said the blonde-headed girl.

"Okay, thanks. One more thing, I didn't catch your names?" I said.

"I'm Katie, that's Josh and the others wouldn't tell us their names. Nice to meet you" She said, smiling.

"Nice to meet you, too" I said.

I went down the hallway on my right and went to the last door.

"Wait; there are two doors on each side! Which one is mine?" I yelled.

"It's the one on the left!" Josh yelled.

I opened the door on the left wall and stepped inside. It was completely empty. It was a small square with a mirror on the side of the wall. The floor was a light brown shag carpet, and the walls were painted gray. It was almost a metallic gray; it had a shine to it. I set my suitcase down on the right side of the wall and looked around.

"Hey! What am I supposed to sleep on here?!" I yelled down the hall.

"Have a pillow! That's all that we have!" yelled Josh, throwing a pillow down the hall.

I don't like that guy. I picked up my pillow and put it on the side of my suitcase. I decided I was going to pile up some clothes and make a makeshift bed. I took out my only dress I had a folded it neatly on the floor. I took some fuzzy pajama pants and put those of top of the dress as a blanket. I felt so poor.

Afterwards, I decided to go back to the center room.

"So, why are you all sitting here?" I asked. "You're all so quiet."

"We don't have anything better to do." Josh said.

"Well, you aren't even talking! How is that better than going outside, or playing a game, or something?" I asked.

"We don't play games. We aren't children." Josh said.

"Well, you could at least talk." I said.

"We are!" He said.

I snorted. He's a little bit of a snob, isn't he? I sat around in the circle for a little bit. Everyone was silent.

"So nobody is going to talk." I said. "You never do and you're not going to change that now."

"We'll talk when something needs to be said." Said the second tallest guy. He had blonde hair. "Right now, something needs to be said and that is, if you don't like being here just leave."

What a group of snobs!

"I will." I said, leaving them and their silent mouths.

I stepped outside and looked around for my favorite tree. I heard a buzzing. I ran to my favorite tree, hoping it was just my ears deceiving me, but I was wrong. The Officials were cutting down my perch. I saw the trunk move, and fall.

"WHAT ARE YOU DOING?!" I yelled to an Official.

"WE ARE REMOVING THIS PESKY TREE. WE NEED TO BUILD MORE HOMES. PEOPLE HAVE FINALLY COME TO THEIR SENSES, AND WANT TO STAY AT THE SQUARE!" He yelled.

I couldn't believe they were doing this. It was only a tree, but there were plenty empty spaces in the Square to build homes! Why would they choose this spot? It wasn't fair! The tree fell to the ground. Well, there goes my perfect spot.

"Why did you choose this spot? There are plenty of other places where you could have built homes!" I said.

"This tree has been in the way for years, we just didn't get a chance to cut it down. This was a perfect opportunity." The Official said.

I scowled at him. I was frustrated with them for tearing down the best thing about the Square. I was already frazzled with my roommates, and now they take away my only spot of peace!

"Humph." I muttered. "What am I doing, I'm being childish. It was just a tree after all."

But it wasn't just a tree. It was a place of solitude, and a place where I could get away from the trouble. I stormed away from the location, huffing and puffing to myself. There wasn't much of a view anymore; everything was block by the houses. I had no other place to go, so I went back to house 142. I went inside, and there they were, sitting around and doing nothing. I went to my room without a word. I flopped on my makeshift bed and laid there for a few minutes. I was so bored; I didn't realize how exhausted I was. I was fast asleep, yet again.

CHAPTER 11: VIVID DREAMER

I was back in the home. I was in the basement. It was pitch black and I couldn't see anything.

"Hey! Stop moving!" A woman whispered, as she grabbed my hand. "We are playing the quiet game, okay?"

I heard a voice upstairs.

"We are looking for a…Penelope?" A man said.

The woman's hand was starting to get sweaty. She was afraid. She muttered something about me.

"…but I have to be here for you Jessica!....No…." She muttered.

"Penelope is dead! She's been dead for years." said another man on the opposite side of the room.

"Our files say she is still alive. You have been lying to us." said the first man.

"No we haven't! You can go look at her tombstone if you don't believe us!" The second man said.

I heard one pair of feet go out the door. I heard a weird electronic noise, and then heard the footsteps return.

"My mistake sir, you were right." The first man said. "Have a good day."

I heard the footsteps leave.

"Wait, make sure they're gone" said the second man's voice. "Okay, the coast is clear. Go get Penelope and Jessica."

I heard footsteps come downstairs. They weren't heavy; it must have been a woman's pair of feet. I heard a door creak open and the light flooded in.

"PERRIE....PERRIE IT'S TIME FOR DINNER!" Josh yelled.

"Wait...what? Oh, COMING!" I yelled.

I keep having these insane dreams! It must be a recurring kind of thing. I quickly pulled myself together, and ran out to the center room. Everyone was still sitting in a circle, but this time, they had food.

"Hello." I said.

"Hey, food is over there." Katie said.

"Thanks." I said, grabbing a plate.

We were having turkey and mashed potatoes. I love turkey! Potatoes are okay, but I just can't find flavor in them, no matter how many seasonings I put on them. I walked over to the spices table and seasoned my turkey with cumin and put a little onion on it as well. I sat down in the center of the circle.

"This is a circle, not monkey in the middle." said one of the brown-haired girls. "Why are you sitting there?"

"I'm sitting here as the center of the conversation. I will make you people talk, whether you like it or not. I need to know more about you all." I said. "Okay, I'm going to play a game. It's your choice to participate or not. I will turn to one of you, and you will tell me something about yourself, or I will throw my mashed potatoes at you."

I spun around on my feet and stopped at the shortest guy. He was silent.

"You have four seconds. I'm really going to do it." I said.

He remained silent, crossed his arms, and stuck his tongue out at me. I threw a handful of mashed potatoes at him. He gasped. I was laughing so hard. His face was hilarious!

"I'm reporting you to the Officials!" He said.

"It talks!" I said.

He was right though, he could report me to the Officials. I would just explain what happened. Surely they would understand.

CHAPTER 12: I WAS KIDDING

The Officials said that I had committed the offense of assaulting a citizen.

"I'm so violent! I'm going to kill EVERYONE with my mashed potatoes." I said sarcastically.

"Do you want another 15 days taken off?" The Official said.

I sighed. "No sir."

"Allright. You don't get to finish your dinner because you used it as a weapon." He said, taking my plate away.

"You can't do that! I am a citizen of the Pure City and am entitled to 3 complimentary meals a day!" I said.

"This is your punishment. If you would like this to be the only one, keep your mouth shut." The Official said, and walked out the door.

I am really starting to not like the Officials.

"I hope you learned your lesson." The "victim" said.

I wanted to kick that guy. Oh wait, sorry, that is an "extremely violent" offense. I sulked all the way back to my room. When I closed the door I heard voices.

"She's hilarious!" Katie said.

I put my ear against the door.

"Maybe, but we don't know her. Should we tell her?" Josh said.

"Not yet. She'll figure it out." Josh said.

I'll figure what out?

"I really feel bad though. She has the right to know what happened. She should come and stay in my room for a while." Katie said.

"NO! She will be the victim and there is nothing we can do about it. Soon, she'll be gone. Don't get too attached." Someone said

What did they mean, I'll be gone? I'm not going anywhere. Wait, I'm going to bed, actually. I didn't feel well at all. I forgot to recharge my spark! I went to the mirror.

"Awake." I said.

"Hello. Input name, please." The mirror said.

This mirror has never been used before.

"Perrie Fawn." I said.

"Hello, Perrie." She said.

"I need my spark recharged." I said.

"Of course." She said, making buzzing and whirring noises. "Authorized."

I felt my chest vibrate, and then I saw my spark come out of my chest. It was as beautiful as ever.

"Is there anything else I can do for you, Ms. Fawn?" She said.

"That will be all." I responded.

I went to my suitcase and put on my pajamas. I pulled my pajama pants over myself, to make sure I was warm on this cold floor. I felt so unprotected. I'm used to sleeping in a sleeping tube, but apparently we don't have those here. I thought about some random things before falling asleep.

CHAPTER 13: PANCAKES AND MYSTERY

I woke up to the smell of something sweet. I heard some chatter in the center room. I got up and got dressed as fast as I could. I knew that smell anywhere. It was pancakes. Pancakes were my favorite breakfast of all time!

"Good morning!" I said in a cheery tone. I love pancakes.

"Good morning." Everyone said groggily.

They all spoke! It was a miracle! I didn't care though; I was too busy drooling over the pancakes on the table. I quickly grabbed a plate and took 3 giant pancakes. I grabbed the whipped cream and smothered it. I went to the basket of fruit and put a bunch of blueberries and raspberries on it. I formed a smiley face. I sat in the circle, like everyone else did. I started to stuff my face, and before 5 minutes were gone, I had horked down 2 pancakes. Everyone was staring at me with a shocked look on their face.

"What?" I said, with pancake still filling my mouth.

One guy rolled his eyes and returned to eating his pancakes. Nobody ate all of the pancakes they took though. They looked sick.

"Are you guys alright?" I asked. I didn't want anyone to throw up on my lap or anything.

"We're fine." Katie said.

"You all look pale. Are you sure you're feeling alright?" I said.

"Actually, we don't feel the best. We suggest you go outside, we could be contagious." Katie said.

"...Well, okay. I don't want to get sick." I said, walking out the door with my pancakes.

When I stepped outside, I realized why they "felt sick". In front of me was a cold, dead corpse. The Officials were standing around it. They weren't examining it though; they were holding the knife that had killed her. The knife was lodged in her chest, and one Official was holding it. I dropped my pancakes and ran back inside.

"WHAT ARE THEY DOING TO HER?!" I whispered although wanting desperately to yell.

"We saw everything." Josh said.

I looked through the peephole in the door. The Officials were standing at our door.

"No time for explaining, they're here! What do we do?" I said.

"There's nothing we can do. The only option is to run, or comply. Unless you want to be killed, I suggest we listen to what they have to say." Josh said.

"But what if they kill us because we saw it!?" I said.

"As I said, there is nothing we can do." Josh said, opening the door.

The Officials stepped inside.

"Hello, is the-"Those were Josh's last words.

The Officials pulled out their guns, and disintegrated Josh. That was enough for me to know I needed to leave, right away. The room turned into chaos. Everyone was running around, looking for escape. I saw Katie motion to me, so I ran to her.

"There is a window in my room, I can open it and we can jump out." She said.

"Okay, but make it quiet and quick, we don't want to be seen." I said.

We slipped away from the chaos and ran quickly to Katie's room. She opened the window, and jumped outside.

"Come on!" She said, looking up at me.

I jumped down and she caught me. She was strong for her size.

"Where are we going to go?" I said.

"Anywhere but here...We should go back to my house in the South Gate. The Officials have stopped patrolling the housing outside the Square." She said. "We are now criminals. We ran away from the Officials, resisting arrest, and whatever other discipline they could impose on us, so we need to go now."

CHAPTER 14: FUGITIVES

We arrived at Katie's house quickly. Thankfully, the Officials hadn't caught up. I felt bad leaving all those people back there to die. I couldn't have done anything anyway though. I can't take any more of this "run away or die" kind of thing. I valued my own life though, so I'm definitely going to keep it for as long as possible.

"Does your T.V. still work?" I asked Katie.

"Yes. I would only turn it on if it is absolutely necessary. The Officials could trace the T.V. and see it's on. They know I was in the housing, so they could find out we're hiding here." She said.

I actually hadn't thought about that.

"I'm only going to turn it on for a few seconds. I want to see if they have labeled us as criminals yet." I said, turning on the T.V.

It started to speak.

"ALERT TO ALL CITIZENS: TWO FUGITIVES HAVE RESISTED ARREST BY THE OFFICIALS AND ARE CRIMINALS. IF ANYONE KNOWS THE LOCATION OF THESE TWO, PLEASE CONTACT THE OFFICIALS FOR AN AWARD." It said, showing our faces on screen.

I turned the T.V. off. I had seen enough. We surely can't stay here at Katie's house the whole time... So what are we going to do?

"Katie, are we going to stay here for a long time? We aren't very far from the Square..." I said.

"We aren't staying here long. We will only stay the night. I need to get a few things before we head out." She said.

"Where are we going to go?"

"A place my father told me about, long ago. Hopefully, it's still there.

CHAPTER 15: LEGENDS AND STORIES

It was late afternoon. I was sitting on the couch, while Katie packed her bags. I still wasn't sure about this whole, "place my father told me about". What was that supposed to mean? Was it even there anymore? What about our sparks? Are there mirrors there? Is it even safe to use a mirror without being tracked? My mind was spinning with questions. I decided to slowly answer them, one by one.

"Katie, are there mirrors at the place we are going to?" I asked.

"Yes." She replied.

"Is it safe to use them without being traced?" I asked.

"No. That's why the house is already full of sparks." She said.

"What do you mean?"

"There are sparks in jars on the shelves. There is an old trick to hacking your heart gate, to authorize spark installations yourself. I will teach you how to do it when the time comes." She said.

Katie is hiding something. I don't know what, but I know it's something. It was time for dinner. I got up and went to the pantry looking for food. All of the cabinets were empty. The only thing in the fridge was a package of bread. I looked around for some butter or something to put on it, but I couldn't find anything. I found an apple in the very back of the fridge. I decided to make apple toast. I put the bread into the toaster, and waited for it to come up. I put the apple into the microwave and warmed it for about 7 seconds. I took it out and mashed it up in a bowl. By the time I was done, the apple was cold. I put the applesauce on the hot piece of toast. It was all we had and I wasn't going to eat toast plain!

"Katie I made some applesauce and we have bread. You can make toast or a sandwich." I said.

"Okay, thanks." She said.

I sat down on the couch and ate the toast. It tasted sweet with the applesauce on it, but it wasn't exactly dinner. It made my stomach a little jumpy because it was so rich. It was actually sickening, but we didn't have anything else. The sun was setting and it was getting dark outside. I didn't know where I was supposed to sleep, so I just decided to sleep on the couch. I was sleeping soon enough, but I got really cold and woke up a few times during the night.

When I awoke, Katie was standing over me holding out a bag.

"Here, this is yours." She said.

"What's inside?" I asked.

"It's just the essentials." She said. "Come on, we need to get going as soon as possible."

"Okay." I said, following her out the back door.

"Follow me." She said.

"There's not much of anything else I can do." I said.

We were in her backyard, and we needed to get out without being seen by anyone. People could still be living in this neighborhood, and we were wanted criminals. Katie motioned for me to go to the fence. When I got there, she started to run towards me. Oh gosh, she wanted me to give her a boost. I had to quickly focus on where she would put her foot, and I had to hold it with my hand. I was like a staircase. She jumped over the fence with my help.

"How am I supposed to get over?" I shouted.

She threw a rope over the fence.

"Okay, that works." I said.

I hoisted myself to the top of the fence and jumped over. Katie was already running across the yard to the other side of the fence.

"We are going to just keep doing this until we reach the river." She said.

The next few jumps I poked myself on the top of the fence. After about 5 yards or so, we got to the river. Katie brought an axe. She went to a small tree and chopped it down. She needed help rolling it to the bank.

"We are going to tie the log to one of the lamp posts so it doesn't float away. Try not to fall into the river." She said.

I went ahead and tied the log to one of the crystal lampposts, and started to cross the log. Katie went ahead of me so she was on the other side already. It was a small birch tree, so it was thin. The water's current was very strong and the log moved back and forth.

"Hurry! The tie is coming off the lamppost!" urged Katie.

I just barely made it. I had to jump. If Katie wasn't there I would've fallen into the river, to be washed away to who knows where. Katie grabbed my hands and pulled me up.

"That was close." She said.

I had never been to the other side of the river. (Well, consciously...) It was so barren. It looked like dried up plains. There were a few trees here and there, and one little pool of water, but other than that, I couldn't see anything but cracked earth.

"This way." Katie said and gestured to me to follow one of the cracks in the ground with her.

"So this place we're going to…. What is it, exactly?" I said.

"It used to be a shelter for anyone who needed it."

"Well, how long ago did your father tell you about it?"

"I was a child. There are many stories about the place, and he would always talk about it."

"What were the stories?"

"Well, considering we are going to be walking for a while, I'll tell you the most well-known." She said. "A long time ago, there was no Pure City. There was only grass and villages. All of 10 villages made up the population of a city. There were 5 cities in all of the Earth. The world had just gone to war, and there weren't a whole lot of people left on Earth. Day by day, people would get sick and die. We needed a cure for the sickness. Every city's people were dying off, so each one scuttled about to make a vaccine. Finally, after a few months of testing, the 3rd city came up with a solution. There were only 2 cities left. All of the others were too late. The 3rd city thought it was better than the other city, so they wouldn't share the vaccine. Eventually, war broke out between the two. The war was violent, and it killed many citizens. Then, someone stood up, and presented a truce. The only people that were left could live in these shelters, while they build a city for all. That is what the shelters are for. The only price they had to pay was a select number of people are used as workers in a new project." She said.

"What was the project?" I said.

"Nobody knows. They were just volunteers, and they worked for the person who came up with the truce." She said. "Oh yeah, and that city they were building? That was the Pure City."

I had never heard that tale before.

"Is it a true story?" I said.

"Yes." She said. "We are coming close to a resting spot. We can take a break from walking there."

I soon knew what she meant. We came across a lean-to against a small oak tree. The tree was healthy, so we must have been near water. I sat down and took a breather. It was hot out here. There were no clouds, only the sun and cracked, dry, boiling hot earth. It didn't help that we were wearing dark clothes either.

"Here, drink this. You need to keep your energy up since you didn't recharge your spark." She said.

"Thanks." I said, drinking the liquid. I almost spit it back up. "Ugh, what is in this stuff?"

"It's pure energy. That's what they use to refill the sparks." She replied.

"Are you sure this is safe?" I said.

"I've done it before." She said.

We were quiet for a few minutes.

"Why are you doing all of this for me? You're taking me along, and helping me." I said.

"You're all I have, now that Josh is gone." She said.

"…I don't mean to pry, but were you two….?" I said.

"That's none of your business." She said, snatching the bottle full of energy out of my hand. "Break time is over, and if you want to stay alive, I suggest we keep moving."

Sheesh, she's touchy. Then again, if they were together, Josh just died. I'm being a bit disrespectful.

"Sorry…" I said to Katie. "I was being disrespectful. If you and Josh were together, I'm sorry, and I won't bring it up again."

She started to sniffle. Oh great.

"We weren't together. I loved him but he didn't love me back. I sacrificed so much for him, but he never saw that." She said, still sniffling.

"You know, that happened to me once. I decided to never fall in love again. I know how you feel." I said.

"You do?"

"Yeah, I do."

"It's nice not to be the only one." She said.

"Tell me about it." I said, giggling. She started to laugh.

We kept on walking until it started to get dark.

"How much farther is this place?" I said. My feet were exhausted.

"It's only a few more miles. We'll get there before it gets too dark. She was right. We arrived just before I couldn't see what was in front of me. Standing in front of us was a small, rotten, wooden shack with one window. The window was cracked and you could see through some of the walls.

"THIS is what the creator of the Pure City, a super talented architect, made for citizens to live in?" I said.

"It's a really old story." Katie said.

We didn't need to unlock anything, the door opened easily. Then again, there was no need for a lock, considering we were in the middle of nowhere.

"How did you know where this shack was?" I asked.

"I memorized the tale, and hoped that the directions were right." She answered.

"So, we could have possibly gotten lost in the search for a fairytale house." I said.

"It was real though!" She said.

I could've gotten lost and died. Thanks a lot Katie.

"Is this all there is to this rinky-dink place? Surely there must be a more secure area!" I said.

"Actually there is. Each one of the houses had a bunker underneath." She said, pressing a button.

I saw the ground shake, and a small outline of a hatch popped up. Katie pulled on it, but it wouldn't open.

"I need your help, it's old and heavy!" She said.

I helped her lift the hatch. Once it was open, she pulled out a portable orb from her bag and flicked the side. The orbs were literally sparks in a ball. When you flick them, they come to life. She threw the orb down the steps and into the bunker. The bunker lit up. It would have been small for a large amount of people, but it was roomy for us. The bunker was in the shape of a pill. The end walls were rounded and had small beds built into them. There was a small kitchen on the right, and a fold out table in the wall to the left. It was really dirty, and in some places there were dead mice… Other than that, it was great for people on the run. I saw an old fashioned looking T.V. sitting on the counter of the kitchen shelf. It was REALLY old though. It had two sticks coming out of the top. I wondered how long we were going to stay here.

"So, how long do you think we'll be here?" I asked Katie.

"However long it takes." She said.

"What do you mean, however long it takes?" I said.

"We'll be here until we are pronounced dead." She said.

"Wait, so are we supposed to fake our death or something?" I said, laughing.

"Pretty much, yes. We'll have to trick the Officials into claiming us dead. Once that is done, we can go under new names, dye our hair, and maybe even cut it off. We're not safe in the City. We never will be again." She said.

"Okay, I'm going to need you to explain some things. You guys saw everything that happened earlier today, didn't you? The Officials were murdering a citizen." I said.

She paused for a moment, losing the color from her face. She looked sick again.

"…Yes. There was a girl sitting outside on her house's doorstep, drinking her coffee. I don't know why, but the Officials came up to her, said something, she refused politely, then they picked her up, dropped her, and then they killed her. She wasn't a criminal. She was innocent. She wasn't resisting arrest or anything. Josh heard half of what they said. He said it was about helping them finish a task. If it was just a task, there was no reason to murder her over it! I don't understand. The city used to be safe. I just don't know anymore. Now that Josh is gone, you're the only other person who has ever been nice to me. I can't lose you too." She said.

She was very clingy. She must have been alone for a long time. I'm the only friend she has left and whether I like it or not, I'm going to have to be here for her. I was getting really tired. My spark hadn't been recharged.

"Hey Katie, one more thing, where are those sparks in the jars?" I asked.

"They're in the cupboard over there." She said, pointing to the cabinet over the sink.

I walked over to the cabinet and opened it up. I saw sparks floating in jars. It was one of the most beautiful things I had ever seen. I took one jar down and held it to my chest. It felt warm in my arms. I looked back in the cupboard. There was only one bad thing about this place so far. There were only 12 sparks. That will last only 6 days, considering there are 2 of us. Let's hope that will be enough.

"Katie, how do you input your spark without a mirror?" I asked.

She walked over to me and opened the jar. The spark started to glow really bright.

"All you have to do is feel your pulse on your wrist, then press." She said.

I found my pulse on my wrist and pressed it. I felt a mechanical whir go through my arm and into my chest. There was a hidden button in my wrist. I felt a shock go from my wrist to my chest. Why is there a hidden button in my wrist that's wired to my heart? Have I always had that? Hm.

The spark came out of my chest and went into the jar with the other spark. The two became one and the spark started to shine.

"This is called a super spark. These will last you 2 days without having to recharge." She said.

"Wow…" I said.

CHAPTER 16: THE SECOND DAY

As soon as I woke up I could only smell dirt and stink. Yep, I wasn't dreaming. I turned to my side and saw Katie had turned on the T.V. and was fiddling with the 2 sticks on top.

"Good morning." She said.

"Mgh…..Hi…" I answered groggily.

I slowly made my way towards the cabinet and opened up the jar with the super spark. I pressed the button in my wrist and felt the buzz in my chest. I saw the spark fly in. I felt so energetic. I ran in a circle a few times to try and get rid of the excess energy, but I felt the same when I was done.

"What are you doing..?" Katie asked.

"Trying to burn off energy" I said really fast.

"Slow down! Try not to burn off the energy; you're making the rush accelerate." She said.

"What's a rush?" I asked.

"It's the energy the super spark gives off. If the level of the rush gets too high, it becomes dangerous to the blood system! Calm down, and take a second to get a hold of yourself." She said, trying to grab my shoulders.

I was running too fast.

"Catch me if you can!" I said, running even faster.

"I'm going to stick you. I'll give you a sedative, if you don't slow down." She said.

I barely even heard what she said. I saw her pull out some sort of gun, and she blew into it. I felt a sharp pain in my neck for a few seconds. I was out before I could pull it out of my neck.

CHAPTER 17: WASTING ENERGY

There she was as soon as I opened my eyes; a frustrated Katie standing over me.

"You done now?" She said sarcastically.

"Yeah. I'm finished" I said.

"Well I hope you're happy, you just wasted 2 good days of energy! That spark was for emergencies only Perrie!"

"Well, you didn't say anything, so I figured it was okay! Next time say something if you don't want me to touch it!"

"Next time, use some common sense!" She yelled.

"Cool it, we have plenty more jars." I said.

"Not enough Perrie. Not enough. If we get low on energy, don't touch my side." She said.

She seemed a little more psychotic than usual. I decided to get up and watch her fiddle with the two sticks on top of the T.V.

"…So… what exactly are those two things?" I asked.

"I really don't know. I've never seen them before. I think I'm going to just call them sticks. I can't get the screen to work, no matter what I do! I think the screen has something to do with the position of these sticks." She said.

She fiddled with them for a long time. I eventually got bored, and opened the hatch.

"NO! DON'T GO OUT THERE!" She said.

"Why? I'm just getting some fresh air." I said.

"The Officials could be waiting for us! Who knows what is up there?" She said.

"Humph… Fine." I said, pouting.

I was so bored. This place had nothing to do. I almost wanted to try and fix the sticks myself; Katie was taking forever with it! I pulled out the foldable table and sat on top of it.

"Get down from there!" Katie said.

"I'm trying to keep myself entertained! I'm extremely bored." I said.

"If you want something to do, come here." She said, pulling out her bag.

"While we were near the river, I caught a few fish for food. If you want something to keep yourself busy, you can start to gut them." She said.

Ew. I had nothing else better to do though.

"Fine." I said, grabbing the bag.

I opened it up and lying in a bag were 5 dead fish. They weren't small either.

"Ew…." I said, picking one up. It felt so slimy.

I opened up the drawers in the kitchen and found a knife. I had never gutted a fish before, actually. This should be interesting. I took one of the fish and set it on a chopping block. I cut off the head first.

"EW!!" I screeched as I heard a small bone crunch. This is nasty.

I proceeded to cut the fish up. I took the knife and slowly sliced down the stomach. I couldn't bare it. It was gross. I saw the skeleton, and threw up.

"PERRIE!" Katie yelled. "If you couldn't handle it you should've told me!"

She furiously went to work on my masterpiece I made on the floor. I didn't feel good at all and decided it would be best to rest for a while. I went over to the sink and washed up. I had to rinse my mouth out and wash my shirt as best as I could. I went over to my bag and found a new clean shirt, and put that on. Before I got into the covers, I went to the sink, filled it up, and put my shirt in there. Katie would finish the washing part for me.

CHAPTER 18: SIGNAL

 It was dark. The lights were off, and there was a small glow from Katie's orb on the kitchen counter. It must have been night time. I saw a small glow coming from the T.V. It's funny; Katie was asleep in the bed on top of me. I heard her snore. Did she leave the T.V. on? I quietly got out of bed. I ran over to the kitchen shelf and grabbed the orb. I hate the dark. I walked over to the T.V. It was turned on, and the picture showed nothing but static. I thought it was my turn to try and fix the stick. I fiddled with one of them. Once I saw the T.V. flash part of a picture. I moved the right stick back to where it was. The picture started to flash more frequently. I started to move the second stick and fiddled with it for a moment. It didn't take long for me to fix it. It was close to its right spot. The picture finally showed up on screen and sound came through. It was loud and I had to turn it down. I saw Katie stir, but she didn't wake up. She continued to snore. On the T.V. was a news reporter. He was talking about a disappearance of a woman. I couldn't hear her name, but I knew they were talking about the murdered girl we saw yesterday morning. I started to wonder if the Officials were behind all of this. They had to be! The question is though, why would the Officials be behind the disappearances? What did they have to do with killing citizens? What was the job they wanted them to do? Surely it wasn't something to kill someone over! Was it? The T.V. started to speak again.

"Officials say that the people responsible for the disappearances are Perrie Fawn and Katie Fitzgerald. If you have seen these two, please contact the Officials right away." The reporter said.

Our faces showed up on screen.

"These two are armed and dangerous. They are criminals. Please, if you have any information about them, contact the Officials right away." He said.

The Officials were lying through their teeth. They know we didn't kill her, but they are going to blame the crime and the disappearances! I think it's now official that I hate the Officials.

"Wait…what?" I said to myself. That sounded much better in my head than it probably would have from my mouth.

I turned my attention back to the T.V. They were broadcasting the weather for tomorrow.

"Tomorrow's weather will be cloudy with a chance of scattered thunderstorms." The weatherman said. "The thunderstorms will have lightning, so we would advise for citizens to stay in their homes."

Lighting and tall crystals do not match each other. If lightning strikes a crystal, it electrocutes anything within a 1 mile radius. Inside our homes, we used to be protected from these surges of power, but now that our security systems are down, well… let's hope there isn't any lightning. I tried to go back to sleep, but my mind just kept talking to me. It kept asking who and why questions. Its curiosity was keeping me awake.

"Shut up." I told myself.

It didn't work. I tossed and turned for a little bit, and realized I was wasting my time. I could be doing something productive. I got up and went back to the T.V. I was going to make sure these sticks didn't move. I needed something to secure them to the top. I looked in my bag, but all I could find was rope, and I don't think I wanted to waste it on some T.V. Since Katie was asleep, I don't think she would mind if I looked in her bag. It was for a good cause. The good cause being, fixing the T.V. that was supposed to be off anyway… I rummaged through her bag.

"Dead fish, rope, orbs, a canister of pure energy… wait, what's this?!" I whispered to myself.

I pulled out a blinking light. It was like a small button, but you couldn't press it and it was blinking red.

"What is this thing..?" I whispered, holding it up.

I looked at the red button again. I put my finger on the light. It spoke back to me.

"Fingerprint invalid. Access denied." It said.

I covered it with my shirt. It was kind of loud. I looked back over at Katie. She stirred. She kept on snoring though. I would've been awake if it were me. She sure is a heavy sleeper. I wondered if maybe it needed her fingerprint… It was worth a shot. I quietly tiptoed across the room, and walked up to the beds built in to the walls. I slightly touched her hand to see if she would move. She flinched just a little, but she didn't move. I put the device up to her finger. The light turned green.

"Fingerprint recognized. Access granted." It said. I hid it under my shirt so it wouldn't make as much noise as it did before. Katie rolled over on her other side and continued to snore. I looked back at the device. It started to blink green this time, instead of red. What was this thing?

It wasn't relevant to the moment at hand though, so, who cares. I'm tired. I guess under pressure I get tired easily. I went to my bed and brought the blinking device with me. I was asleep pretty quick.

CHAPTER 19: BETRAYAL

I woke up to a gun pointed at me. I struggled to get out of bed, but my hands and feet were tied.

"I knew I couldn't trust you." Katie said.

"What do you mean?!" I said.

"Where did you put it?" She said.

"PUT WHAT?!" I screamed. I had no idea what was going on.

"The device!" She said.

"WHAT DEVICE?! THE BLINKING ONE?!!" I yelled.

"YOU KNOW WHICH ONE IT IS. GIVE IT BACK." She said.

"ONLY IF YOU TELL ME WHAT IT IS AND WHY YOU HAD IT!" I said.

"Okay, fine. I'll make this easy for you. Give me the device, or I'll be the last thing you ever see." She said, with a snarly tone in her voice.

"I thought you were my friend! Why would you murder me over some blinking button?!" I said.

"It's not just a button you idiot! That was a homing device. I had it with me only for emergencies. If one of us got lost or taken, I could use that to send you a signal so you could find me and vice-versa. The only bad thing about it is that once you turn the signal on, you broadcast it to ANYONE who has a receiving device. You had one in your side pocket of your bag. Josh had one. Every single solitary Official has one. You've just broadcasted our location to them!" She said. "Give me the device so I can disarm it! For all I know, you could be working for the Officials!"

She was afraid, and was jumping to conclusions. I kicked the device out of the bed, where I had hidden it.

"Okay, calm down, you're jumping to conclusions. Think about it. Am I really working for the Officials? Why would I have run away with you to this location if I was working for them?" I said.

"If you're not with the officials, why do you have one of these!?" She said, pulling out my compact mirror.

"That's a compact-"I said, but I was interrupted.

"A compact homing device disguised as a mirror. Watch this." She opened the mirror. "Mirror, find homing signal.

The mirror responded, and started beeping. She showed me the screen. It was beeping with a sonar-like tracking program. I didn't even know that compact mirrors had that capability!

"Since you've broadcasted our location to your co-workers, why don't I leave you here so they can find you? They could possibly blame you for the murder of that woman, but it doesn't matter to me. I'm getting out of this alive." She said, grabbing her bags.

She dropped the device in front of the bed.

"I hope you enjoy your sentence of death!" She said, opening the hatch and running out the door.

I was in serious trouble. I knew the Officials were coming. I needed to move. That homing device was on all night. They could already be here, for all I know! I wiggled my way out of my bed and fell onto the floor. I fell on my back.

"Ouch." I said.

I needed to get the ties off my feet and hands, quickly. The knives were in the kitchen, and Katie could've taken them. I wasn't sure though, and it was worth a shot. I inch-wormed my way to the kitchen. I went as fast as I could, getting rug burn from the carpet on the floor. I made my way to the kitchen and I had to get myself up somehow. I tried rolling around to get myself into a somersault so I could end up on my feet. It didn't work out so well. I hit the counter and knocked over the T.V. The glass screen cracked, and the picture went black.

"Well looks like the T.V. and the floor got married. The reception is terrible so far." I said.

I crack myself up. Since the rolling around idea didn't work, I decided to try and pull myself up. My hands weren't free, but my arms were. I reached up to a kitchen counter and tried to grab it with my hands. I missed and feel back onto my back. That was a little painful… I tried again, and this time I grabbed the shelf. I used all my strength to pull myself upwards. I finally was on my feet. I had to hop without falling. If I fell, my head would hit the counter and that would end in a bloody mess. I slowly hopped my way to the knife holder. I used my mouth to hold the edge of the knife. This was dangerous. I had to drop the knife in the middle of the ties binding my hands. I started to shake. I could seriously injure or save myself at this moment. I spread my hands apart as far as I could. My mouth let the knife go.

"Ouch!" I said, as the knife slightly cut my wrist. It wasn't anything major, just a sliver of skin was bleeding. I caught the knife before it fell on my foot with my left hand. I cut the band that was tying my feet, and stuck the knife in my bag. It could come in handy for later. I opened the cabinet where the sparks were. The cabinet was empty. I was going to run out of energy. I opened the fridge, and found an apple. Hopefully that would get me through before I could find another spark. If not, I was going to have to use my compact mirror.

"Wait, I don't have that anymore!" I said to myself. "She took it! That's just great…"

Now I had to make a choice:

I needed to find a place nearby, or find my way back to the city. I was going to take my chances looking for the city. I felt I had no other choice. I grabbed my bag and opened the hatch. I didn't know when the Officials could arrive. They could be outside already, waiting for me. I went upstairs and looked for an alternative exit. I looked around, and all that was here was the window to the side that was broken, and the walls that were splitting apart. I saw one of the wall's boards was split aside quite a bit. It looked like this could have been the route Katie took. I looked through one of the holes in the front door. I didn't see anyone standing outside. I looked through the split boards in the back of the house. There wasn't anyone standing there either. I took the knife out of my bag, and stuck it in my pocket, just for safe keeping. I thought it wouldn't have been the best idea to go out the back boards. Something told me it could have been a trap. I opened the front door, just a tad. Nothing happened. I stepped outside underneath the little awning of the house. Still, nothing happened. I walked out into the sunlight. I heard something on the roof, and turned around.

"Freeze" The Official commanded!

.

CHAPTER 20: CAUGHT

I looked at the top of the roof and saw Katie sitting in handcuffs and there was tape on her mouth. The Official jumped off the roof, still pointing his gun at me.

"I said, freeze." He said.

I put my hands up. This man was large. There was no way I would be able to get away from him.

"Get on the ground. I was sent here to collect you two, and to bring you to justice." He said, with a smirk on his face.

I did as I was told. I felt the cold handcuffs go around both of my hands.

"Where are you taking us?" I said.

"No time for talk. Your questions will be answered later." He said, pulling out some tape and putting it over my mouth.

"Mmfh! Mhmmf…" I said, struggling to get the tape off. It was hard to breath.

He grabbed my arm and pulled Katie off the roof.

"Mmmh" She said. It sounded like she said ouch.

He grabbed both of our arms and led us to the back of the house. He tied our feet up. He dropped us on the ground, and got out a button. When he pressed it, a ship came into view. He opened the side door and dragged us inside. It was like a prison cell, with two sets of seats on each side. He shoved us onto the seats and closed the door. It was pitch black for a second. I heard what sounded like a motor, and we started to move. Some lights came on. We were starting to ascend into the air. I heard a few mechanical pops, and then I looked up. Some sort of gas was coming out of what looked like the speakers. I tried to cough, but I couldn't because of the tape over my mouth. I inhaled the gas through my nose, and fell asleep.

CHAPTER 21: PRISON

When I awoke, I was sitting in a prison cell. It was dark, and there weren't any lights. I had a small window at the top of my cell. There was glass in front of me as a door. I stood up realized I was wearing a prison uniform. I felt in my pockets. My knife was gone. They took my bag too. I was sitting on a bed. The glass in front of me had two buttons to the side. One said night and the other said day. I pressed the day button. The glass became see through, and my whole entire cell revealed glass windows and walls. I could see everyone and everything. The prison had cells stacked on top of each other. There were two towers of cells on each side. It felt like a giant glass castle; except it was a castle for criminals. I looked at the cell underneath me. It was a little girl. She didn't look very old either, maybe about 9 years old.

"Hey!" I yelled to her.

She didn't hear me.

"Hello... Up here!" I said, banging on the glass floor.

She looked up at me. She tried to jump towards me and started to say something. I couldn't hear her. It almost looked as if she was crying for help. I put my hand up to the floor and she looked up at me. She started to cry. I felt bad. What kind of person would lock up an innocent child! She isn't even eligible for prison!

I sat all alone in my cell. I wanted my trial, so I could say what really happened. If the Judge would listen, that is. I sat on my cell bed. I was getting hungry. I looked around some more through the cell walls. To the back of me was the North Gate. It was just a field with a lot of Officials standing guard. I saw a small building to the left. It looked like a courthouse. That must have been where they hold the trials. I saw a few guard towers at the entrance of this glass prison. Other than that, it was foggy and I couldn't see much. I looked through the right side of the wall and saw only more cells. These cells were empty though. Only the ones to my right were full of people.

After what seemed like forever, someone came by my cell with a tray full of food.

"Here, you filthy slob." She said, opening a small door and kicking the food to me.

Rude.

Wait, I have a question. When is my trial? My name is Perrie Fawn." I said.

She pulled out a glass tablet. "Your trial is in 10 hours. You've been here for two days; you should know the regular protocol! Everyone is taught this in their first year of school." She said.

Actually, I didn't know the protocol.

"Okay, thanks." I said, closing the door.

I pressed the night button; I didn't like how the other prisoners were staring at my food. I had a ham and cheese sandwich with 4 pieces of broccoli on the side. I didn't get any desert with it. The glass walls became dark and the window above me became the only source of light. I almost forgot to get the water the guard let me have. I started to eat my way through the ham and cheese sandwich, thinking about what I should say in my trial tomorrow. It was night at the moment and by the time my 10 hours were up, it would take place it would be morning. I felt full halfway through the sandwich, but I decided to keep eating. I needed the energy. I had already missed one charging session for my spark, and I need to stay as sane as possible. I ate the rest of the sandwich and started to eat the broccoli. Broccoli is my favorite vegetable. I wish they had given me more of it…

Once I had finished eating, I pressed the day button on my cell wall. I saw that everyone else had their cells in night mode. I looked to the back window, and it was deep into the night. The moon was above my cell. How long did it take me to eat? Once my cell lit up, the same Official came to my cell again and opened the small door.

"Give me your tray." She said.

I gave it to her.

"Alright, now get to bed. You are going to wake up early tomorrow for your trial." She said. She then closed the door.

My spark was running low on energy, and so was I. I needed to try and get some rest to refill whatever energy there was left in the spark. I waddled over to my cell bed. It wasn't really a bed when you think about it. It was more of a slab of glass that was just put there to make our naps miserable. I went over to the cell wall and pressed the night button. Since there was no daylight, it was pitch black in my cell. I bumped into the right wall before I tripped and fell onto the "bed". I tried to get as comfortable as possible, and laid my head on my arm. I was extremely low on energy so I was out like a light.

CHAPTER 22: TRIAL

When morning had awakened me, I saw the small patch of sunlight coming from the small window above me. When I pressed the day button, I saw two Officials standing outside my door. They pressed a few buttons on the outside, and then stepped in.

"We're here to take you to your trial." A woman said.

"Take this spark so you don't run out of vitality. Our statistics showed you were poor in health because of depleting energy." A man said, handing me a spark.

"Authorized spark input." He said into his compact mirror.

I felt the whir in my chest, and the spark flew inside me.

"Now, if you'll come with us…" The woman said.

I felt them put the handcuffs on me. They opened the door and we stepped onto a little platform. The platform had a small steering wheel and railings. The woman took hold of the steering wheel and made the platform go down. We descended to the ground, and they took me through the front door of the prison. I saw Officials standing guard everywhere. They all looked at me as I was escorted to the courthouse. When we got outside, it was sunny. I had to squint my eyes because it was so bright. They marched me to the courthouse. It wasn't as far away as it seemed up in my cell. Before I knew it, we were at the steps of the courthouse. It was actually a large building up close. There were pillars on the left and right of the entrance and a dome on the roof. When we stepped inside, I had to go through to a room and wait until my name was called.

"Perrie Fawn." A speaker said. "You're trial is next."

I was escorted by two Officials into the court room. I was put in front of the Judge. I had to swear to tell the truth.

"Do you swear to only tell the truth, and nothing but the truth?" Said the Official.

"I swear…" I said.

I saw a reporter come up to the center of the room with a cameraman behind him.

"The trial for Perrie Fawn is starting, everyone take your seats! This should be interesting!" He said, with a smile. Apparently, I was on live T.V.

The Judge came into the room.

She hit her gavel on a small wooden block.

"Alright, today we are here to review the actions of Perrie Fawn. Perrie Fawn was a nice girl who did everything she was told, until she decided to go rogue. She murdered Camellia Victor, resisted arrest multiple times, and is disrespectful to the Officials. She doesn't care about rules." She said.

None of that was true.

"We have a witness of the crime here with us today." She said.

An Official stood up.

"I saw Perrie Fawn commit the crime of murdering Mrs. Victor. It was morning, and Mrs. Victor was sitting on her porch. She was drinking her coffee, and enjoying life. Perrie came along, pushed her to the ground, and killed her with a knife. We have the knife as evidence here with us today. It contains Ms. Fawn's fingerprints." The Official said, handing another Official the knife.

"Perrie, what is your side of the story?" The Judge asked.

"My side is the only truthful one here. The Officials are framing me. They were the ones who killed Mrs. Victor. I had witnesses who saw it happen too, but the Officials killed them. We knew too much, so I had to run away. We were all claimed criminals." I said.

"Who is "we"?" She asked.

"Katie Fitzgerald and the rest of my housemates in house 142." I replied.

The Judge whispered something to an Official. The Official whispered something back to her.

"Since you were part of the gang of criminals in house 142, we are going to sentence you to the same sentence as Katie Fitzgerald. You will be shipped off to serve your time in a new project that is taking place. You swore to tell the truth and you lied. This is your sentence. Case closed." The Judge said, hitting her gavel on the small block of wood.

"But, that's not-" I said.

"You have no right to speak anymore, the case is closed." The Officials behind me said. "You will be transported to the work site tonight."

These trials were unfair, and they weren't performed right. What about my witnesses? Katie was a witness. I had a right to speak, and I didn't get it when I should have. I bet that the Judge was being bribed with money to give me a sentence like that.

CHAPTER 23: TRANSPORT

I was quickly escorted back to my cell. When we arrived, they pushed me inside, but didn't remove my handcuffs.

"Hey, you didn't remove my handcuffs!" I said.

"It doesn't matter. Where you're going they won't be removed anyway." The Official said, laughing.

I don't understand what they meant. What was this place I'm going to? What is this new project? I've never heard of it before. If there were some sort of new project going on to benefit the citizens, wouldn't they have told the city about it? I didn't like the feeling I was getting by thinking about it.

I tried to sleep. I really did. There was a sound outside that was disturbing me though. It sounded almost as if a low wind sound mixed with a Wolfine's howl. Wolfine were the wild crystal dogs that the Pure City originally meant for protection for the citizens. They didn't like being in captivity, and decided to escape into the wilderness. They hate humans. They are very hard to find, but once in a while, you can hear their distant howls. The howls mixed with wind were giving me chills. Not to mention it was cold anyway, but still. I got up and made my way towards the buttons. I pressed the day one and the walls opened to glass again. It was a crescent moon tonight. I peered down at the Officials guarding on the night shift. One of them was asleep and the other was trying to wake him up. It was quite entertaining to watch. First he tried to kick him, but that didn't work. He was franticly looking at his watch the whole time. He was probably checking to see when another Official would come to check on them. If one of them was asleep, they would have days taken off their Light Cards. The Official ran to go do something, and he came back with a bucket. He poured the bucket full of water on the other Official's head. THAT woke him up.

"Ha-ha!" I said, laughing. Now they were yelling at each other. The sleeping Official was yelling at the other for waking him up, and the first Official was trying to explain. They reminded me of an old married couple arguing over silly little things.

It was really cold in the cell. I guess they didn't have heat for the "filthy slobs". Since the walls were solid concrete and glass, it made the cell even colder. I was shivering. There were no blankets, no pillows, only the clothes on my back. My hair was short so I couldn't have the joy of feeling the warmth of long hair covering my shoulders.

I curled myself up into a ball on the floor. I was freezing. I closed my eyes and decided to ignore the chill on the outside of my clothes. I tricked my mind into thinking that I was warm. It worked only long enough for me to go to sleep.

I woke up to the same routine as yesterday; two officials were standing over me, with an escort waiting outside. They grabbed my arm and started to lift me up.

"I've got this, I'm fine." I said, nudging my arm away from them.

They led me onto the small platform again, but this time, instead of going down, we went up. The platform started to rise and accelerate. I fell because it was going so fast. These prison cells seemed to go on forever. When we came to a sudden stop, I hit my head on the floor. They grabbed my arms again and pulled me up. In front of me was a transport. It was like the vehicle the Official used to take me to the prison. They shoved me inside. This transport was nicer than the one the other Official had. This one had small windows we could look through. It was much roomier on the inside as well. I walked over to a seat. Katie sat on the opposite side of me. There were a few other prisoners sitting in the transport. One of them was fiddling in his seat, and his face was pale white.

"Hey…you okay?" I asked him.

"Oh! Me…Yes, I'm fine. I'm just a little nervous." He said.

"What about?" I asked.

"Wait until they close the door." He said.

He was kind of…strange. We were just going to work on a new project. What is so nerve-wracking about that? The Officials put the last prisoner on the transport and closed the door. I heard the motor-like sound, and we ascended into the air.

"So…what are you so nervous about?" I asked the guy.

"It's funny. Everyone thinks we are being sent to "work on a new project." He said. "It's true; if you consider the "new project" working at a death camp."

"What?!" I said.

"We are being sent to work on a new project. Project Death Camp, as I like to call it. PDC is what's behind the disappearances. The Officials have been slowly killing off humans. I don't know why, but that's what I've heard about this place." He said.

"Who have you heard this from?" I asked, just so I could verify its truth.

"People on the street…they say that they've worked there before, but they escaped alive." He said.

"Okay…" I said.

This guy wasn't telling the truth. If he was, then why haven't those citizens taken the information to the media? I'm only going to believe what I see. I turned my attention to Katie. She was avoiding me.

"So, who's working for the Officials again?" I asked.

"Shut up." She said.

"Oh, I'm sorry; did someone make a false assumption?" I said.

"I said, SHUT UP. Look, I may have been wrong, but right now is not the time to discuss false assumptions. We need to get out of here, right now." She said.

Pssht. Sorry, your majesty.

"…Look, I'm sorry. I-"I said, but I was interrupted.

"No. I'm sorry. It's my fault I didn't tell you about that homing device. We wouldn't be in this situation if it weren't for me. I did make a false accusation and I apologize. I was scared, confused, and I wasn't thinking straight." She said.

I sighed. "I know. I'm sorry for poking at you about it. By the way, why, exactly, do we need to get out of here? We're just going to work on a project for the Officials…" I said.

"I've heard some rumors about the disappearances too. I know that this place is behind them. I know the Officials are taking people to this location, but I don't know what they are doing or where they are going. All I know, is no-one comes back." She said. We're starting to descend and we need to move."

Why is it that I've been in a life or death situation since about a week ago? She was right though, we were starting to descend. She started to panic.

"We NEED to move! Help me get these off! WE'RE GOING TO DIE!" She screamed.

"Calm down! We're not going to be able to get out of this. There's nothing we can do. The best things to do in an emergency are calm down, stop, and think." I said.

She was silent for the rest of the flight. We landed, shortly after that conversation. Some Officials opened up the transport door. I looked outside. It was dusty, but it seemed like the middle of nowhere. We were marched outside and told to stay put for a second. I looked back at Katie. She was stopping herself from speaking.

"Katie, calm yourself, we're okay. Everything's okay." I whispered.

"No. We're going to die." She whispered back. "We need to leave."

"No, Katie, it's not safe. Don't move. Stay with me." I whispered, tearing up. She was going to run.

"No." She whispered, and ran away into the dust.

"HEY! THAT PRISONER IS ESCAPING!" An Official said. He ran after her

A slight tear ran down my cheek.

"LET HER. She won't escape." Another Official said, with a smile on his face.

"Oh, that's right! Ha-ha!" The first Official said.

The second Official stood in front of us, and started to speak.

"ALLRIGHT. YOU PEOPLE ARE HERE TODAY, TO HELP US WORK ON A NEW PROJECT. THE PROJECT TAKES PLACE UNDERGROUND. YOU ARE MINING. YOU AREN'T LOOKING FOR ANY CERTAIN KIND OF MINERAL OR GEM. YOU ARE JUST MINING TUNNELS FOR US. YOU WILL SPEND ALL YOUR TIME DOWN THERE, AND YOU WILL NOT COME BACK UP. DOES EVERYONE UNDERSTAND?" He said.

Everyone was silent.

"ALLRIGHT. GRAB YOUR PICKAXE, AND GET TO WORK. THIS WILL BE THE LAST TIME

YOU'LL BE OUTSIDE, UNTIL YOU FINISH YOUR JOB. IT'S PITCH BLACK DOWN THERE, SO TAKE AN ORB WITH YOU. GOOD LUCK." He said, with a smirk on his face.

I didn't like this at all. It didn't feel like they would take us all the way out here to mine. We were all pushed into a line. We were marched forward for a short distance, and then turned left. We marched left shortly, and reached a mine entrance. At both of our sides were mine carts with our names on them.

"FIND THE MINECART WITH YOUR NAME, AND GET TO WORK." The Official said.

I turned to the mine cart next to me. It wasn't mine. I looked around and checked each cart. None of them were mine. I finally checked the second cart on the right, and thankfully, it was mine. It had a dirty helmet with a light, a rusty pickaxe, and a flare.

"What's the flare for?" I asked.

"If the mine collapses, and if you're still alive, shoot the flare up so we can see you." The Official said.

"Has the mine collapsed before?" I asked.

"No time for any more questions. ONCE YOU HAVE YOUR THINGS, HEAD INTO THE MINES." The Official said.

We were pushed into a line again and marched into the mine. I was at the very back of the line. I heard some chatter from those who had already entered, but I couldn't make out what they were saying. When I entered the mine, the Officials behind us closed the doors. I realized they weren't normal doors; they were heavy duty stronghold doors. I could finally hear what the people in front of me were saying.

"Hey, this isn't a mine! Where are we?!" One person said.

"I don't know! It's pitch black!!" Said another.

I heard a screechy sound come from a speaker.

"Alright, you have likely realized that you are not in a mine. You were right. Your "new project" you must work on is to survive. You will use your pickaxe as a weapon. It is pitch black here. Everyone walk forward 5 big steps, and you'll begin your project." The speaker said.

I took five big steps. It was pitch black. There was no light. I couldn't see my hands in front of me. I grabbed my headlight, and turned it on. It didn't help all that much. All I saw in front of me was the dirt ground. I heard a scream to my left.

"WHAT IS THAT THING?!" I heard a girl say. She screamed.

I was shaking all over. Not only was I afraid of the dark, but I'm also afraid of anything that lives in the dark. I didn't even want to think about it.

Katie and that boy were wrong. This was not a death camp. This was just a death sentence. I heard someone else scream. I ran away from it all until I couldn't hear anything but my footsteps on the ground. I slowly walked forward. I tripped on a twig and fell on my face. My pickaxe fell out of my hand. I heard a snarl. This particular type of snarl was not human, I could definitely tell that. I didn't move. I slowly reached for my pickaxe, but when I tried to move, it snarled some more. I think it could see in the dark. I had two choices. I could run, or I could try to fight whatever it was with my bare hands. I'd rather not get my head chewed off by some creature of the night, so I decided to run. I got up as fast as I could and I ran. I heard it come after me. It had a big huff in its breath; it must have been large.

"No! Please!" I said as I was running.

I heard everything go silent for a moment. It had stopped running. I turned around, and I couldn't see anything there. I looked around, trying to think what happened.

"Where did you go…?" I said.

I knew it would be back soon, wherever it went, so I kept on running. The moment I started to run, I heard the snarl again. This time, I ran into its face. It was big, slimy, and furry. It tried to bite me, but I jumped back before it could. I looked at it with my light. I will never sleep with my lights off again.

PART 2: THE GLOAM

CHAPTER 24: LIFE IN THE GLOAM
Otto

I was walking in the forest, doing my usual scouting.

I couldn't find where she went, but I didn't want to go risking my life for her. The forest was a dark, dense, creepy place where the creatures lived. If you don't go inside, the creatures won't really come out looking for you. I heard a soft meow, and followed it. This little thing had wandered far from the camp. The meow was getting slightly louder. It almost sounded like it was in pain. I finally found it, stuck in a thistle patch. I got my wooden knife out and started to slowly cut the thorny branches.

"Don't worry little one. I'm going to get you out. Shhh. I won't hurt you." I said, as it looked at me with wide eyes.

I finally cut the branch that was holding her leg. Her leg was slightly bleeding, so I tore off a piece of my shirt and wrapped it around it. I turned to the kitten and started to speak. She was meowing.

"What do you want from me….Bo?" I said. Bo seemed like a nice name. I shouldn't name things I'm not going to keep though.

"Mew." She said, rubbing against my leg.

"You're adorable. I don't need any more mouths to feed though." I said.

"MEW. MEW." She said, jumping onto my jacket.

She was too sweet. I needed someone sweet in my life.

"Okay, fine, but you won't get a TON of food." I said.

I picked her up and she started to cling to my chest. Then, she climbed onto my shoulder and was purring.

I took out the wooden knife again, and started to roam through the forest. I was hungry, and now I had another mouth to feed. I needed some company after that boy went missing. He never talked to me, he wouldn't even LOOK at me, but I fed him and one day he disappeared. He probably got curious and decided to follow me into the forest. That was a bad idea for an inexperienced one. He'd probably been taken by one of the creatures. I heard a rustle in the trees above me. I stopped. I couldn't see anything, but I could hear movement above me. It could be one of two things. It could have been a Brid, a delicious, fox-eared, white wing-tipped bird that was delicious to eat. Or, it could have been the other creature. I haven't heard of a name for them, but they are like cats and pterodactyls combined. I was hoping for the Brid. I drew my knife close, and looked for a slight glow in the darkness. Anything light colored would stick out, just a little. I heard a squeal. It was a Brid! I heard wing movements coming closer, and I ducked. The Brids have very sharp beaks; if you got too close, it could cut you. I heard a wing movement coming closer from behind, so I ducked again. It was going to come in for another attack, so I waited until I heard movement. I heard the last wing movement it would make before flying off; I only had one shot at this. I heard the flapping wings come closer and closer, and I threw my knife in front of me.

"SQUACK!" It said.

I felt feathers hit my feet. I hit my target. I took out my sack, and shoved the dead Brid inside. I felt the kitten dig its claws into my shoulder.

"Ouch!" I said. She was trembling with fear. I had almost forgotten she was there. I pet her head, to reassure her, and soon she was purring again. I had dropped my orb in the process of hunting, so I picked it up and held it again. I needed to get out of the forest and back to my campsite. I felt around for the nearest tree, and put Bo inside my bag. I sealed it so she couldn't get out. She started to meow again.

"It's alright; I'm just concerned for your safety." I told her. I put the orb in my mouth, and started to climb up the tree. It wasn't a tall tree, but it was enough to see over the others. Once I got to the top, I looked for a faint glow in the darkness. To my right, I saw a red-yellow glow. I saw a gray stack of mist coming up from above it. That was the fire I had set, so I could find my way back. I remembered the direction, climbed down the tree and headed towards it. I couldn't run or I could run into a tree, but I jogged as fast as I could to my campsite. I heard a few growls to my side once, but I didn't pay attention. The creatures look for runners; it attracts them. Whenever you're first put in the Gloam, the people who run and scream are the ones who get killed first. Unfortunately, that is a lot of people.

I finally got to my fire. It was starting to burn out, so I needed to make another. I carried Bo up to my makeshift house, and found a small box.

"This is your house. I don't want you wandering off, so I'll close the box at night. I'll make you a yard and a fence so you don't run off, okay?" I said, petting her head. She was still purring.

I took the orb out of my bag, where I had placed it when I was climbing up my tree. It had automatically turned itself off, to save power. I tapped it once, and it put out a dim light. It was just enough to light up my tree. I found my blanket, and padded it into the box. I set Bo in the box, and closed one of the flaps. I tore off a small branch for her to play with.

"There you go." I said, giving her the stick.

Her tail was flicking and her eyes got huge. She pounced on the stick and started to gnaw on it.

"Good girl." I said. I pulled a small stick of wood out of my sack, and took out the rock. I have used this rock for a couple of years, and it had a bunch of chips taken off it, but it still served its purpose.

"Stay here." I told the kitten. It was a big box I had given her, she wouldn't leave.

I climbed down to the ground, and started the fire again. I saw a creature snarl and go away. I hadn't seen that type of hybrid before. Maybe it was a new breed…? I don't know. I took out the Brid and hung it over the small fire. I love Brid. I was lucky to find one. A few years ago, this area was full of them. They were flying all over the place; their ears were turned down, as they should be. Now, their ears are turned upwards, and they are really scrawny looking. All of the creatures were changing. It almost seemed as if one species disappeared, and a new one came into place.

The Brid was finished cooking in a few minutes. It was a small one, so it didn't take long to get it nice and brown. I took out my pickaxe and chopped it in half. I went back up the tree, taking my stone and stick with me, and went to my makeshift home. I gave the kitten a leg of the Brid, and gave myself the rest. That leg would feed her for a long time. I wondered how she got in here! You only get sent to the Gloam by the Officials. Maybe someone had snuck her in with them, only to find out that this was a place of death, and not a place of life. Her owner was probably killed by the monsters that guard the entrance to the REAL Gloam.

After a while, I heard tiny snores coming from Bo. She was so cute when she slept. I closed her box, and put a rock on top, so she wouldn't go anywhere. She relieved herself, so she should be fine. I looked up at the blackness above me. I wondered what was up there. Was it the ceiling of the earth above us? Or did the darkness go on and on forever. I didn't know and I never would. I took my extra blanket out of a hole in the trunk of the tree, and was about to go to sleep myself, until I heard a voice.

"No! Please!" It said. It sounded like a girl. I hadn't heard another human voice for quite some time.

"Where did you go…?" She said.

She wasn't far away. I could hear a snarl too. She must've been in some trouble. I could use some human company.

"Stay here." I told Bo.

She stuck her paw through one of the holes and smacked my hand.

"Hah! Kittens." I exclaimed!

I grabbed my wooden knife and climbed down the tree. I grabbed the orb from the tree and listened for the girl again. I heard the snarl from the creature, and ran towards it. I threw the orb, and it hit the girl.

"OUCH!" She said, falling to the ground.

Oops.

I saw the outline of the creature. It was looking at the orb. It walked a little closer to it, and ran away. The creatures didn't like the light. I ran to the outline of the fallen girl, and looked at her face. She was beautiful. Her face was so perfect. I picked her up, and picked the orb up too. I went back to the tree as fast as I could. I couldn't carry her up the tree though, she was too heavy. I set her down at the base of the tree, and put the orb back in its place. I heard a meow from the box. I wanted to go back up in my tree, where it was safe, and sleep. I couldn't just leave her here for the creatures to find… So I decided to stay with her until she woke up. I fell asleep, watching her.

When I awoke, it was pitch black again. I heard a snarl right in front of me. THE FIRE WAS OUT! I had fallen asleep and I hadn't made a new one! I looked up in the tree and still heard small snores coming from Bo, who was still asleep. I looked down at the girl; she was still asleep too. I felt around for my orb, but I had left it at the top of the tree. Whenever I started to move, I heard a growl from the creature in front of me. I looked down at the girl asleep. If she didn't move, the creature would be less inclined to attack her. If I could wake her up, explain what's going on, distract the beast, and she would lie still, I could get her out of here safely! All plans aside though, I didn't know this girl. She was just another soul to take care of and another mouth to feed. Even if she is pretty, I couldn't just let her into my family! I let the kitten into mine because it had stayed alive for what seemed like weeks and she would always know where I was. I didn't think it was a good idea to help the girl if I could lose my life, but I had an idea. I tore off a piece of bark from the tree and waved it around at the creature. The creature stopped, and started to glow a little. What the heck was this thing? When the creature lit up, it showed its facial features and its stature. It almost looked like a wolf and an alligator. It had the face of a wolf, the feet and scales of an alligator, a dog's ears, nose, and tail. Its eyes had yellow pupils with a black ring inside. It wasn't the cutest thing in the world. It was actually mildly disturbing. When I waved the stick, its tail wagged a little. Maybe the dog in it wanted to play…? I moved the stick to the other side of him. It growled again. I was going to take a hunch. I threw the stick, and it ran after it, barking and growling. As I said before, the creatures are less inclined to attack things that aren't moving. I tried to lift the girl, but when she was sleeping, she was heavy. I could pick her up before, so, what's the deal?! I couldn't risk anymore time though. It was either me or her. If she was asleep it would be painless. I quickly climbed up my tree and turned on the orb. I heard the growling creature coming back. I then heard her scream. That wasn't so bad…I fell asleep in guilt. I can't believe I was that heartless to an innocent girl.

CHAPTER 25: IN THE BELLY OF THE BEAST
Perrie

I felt a bite on my leg. I was in someone else's arms when I woke up. I couldn't see a face, but the hands felt masculine. He was lightly stroking my hair. It was creepy. I heard a growl though, and froze. I had just been chased by one of those, and I think it found me again. My heart started to beat faster. I heard the beast growl. I think it could see in the dark; it saw me. I heard the boy above me pull a piece of what sounded like bark off of something. His arm started to move, but I couldn't see what he was doing. Judging by the movements in his arm, he just threw something. After the growling was gone, he left me and started to climb up a tree. I knew it was a tree by the way the branches and leaves rustled. I heard a mew too. Where was I? I sat up, and rubbed my head. It was throbbing for some reason. I looked around and still couldn't see anything. By the time my head was done throbbing and I had gotten my senses back, the growling was coming back. It was getting closer and there were two growls coming from two monsters. I felt something scaly brush my leg and I felt it bite my leg. I screamed. The pain didn't last long though, because there weren't any teeth.

"Huh?" I said.

I felt extremely sick all of the sudden. They had poisoned me with their gums. This place was a nightmare come true. I almost threw up, but my stomach wouldn't let me. I felt a burning in my throat, and I went completely blind. I couldn't see much before, but I did see a faint outline of things. Now, All I could see was black. I felt something around my leg again, but this time it was pulling me. I guess they only use their mouth for poisoning and…well…I don't want to think about it. I was dragged across a lot of branches, and once across a thistly patch. We came into a stone area, my guess it was a cave. The monster let go of my leg. I tried to move my arm, but it was hopeless. I was paralyzed. I couldn't move anything. I was panicking. What if this was the end of me? I heard a spine-tingling crunch. It sounded like a bone… It was most likely an animal's bone. It was only an animal's bone. I tried to call out for help, but I couldn't move my mouth either. At least I wasn't going to see what was going to kill me. Even though I was blind, I could still feel and I felt a warm source nearby. It was like that feeling you get from sitting by a fire, but it wasn't a fire. Sometimes light gives off that type of heat. What was it? I felt the ground move slightly too. They were steps, but I couldn't tell if they were human or monster. I felt the warmth get closer. It was like a fire was moving towards me. It frightened me that I couldn't see what it was. As it got closer, I realized it wasn't anything hostile. It was so close I felt I could touch it. I tried to move my arm, and I could. I could only move it just a little, but that was good! The effects of the poison were wearing off. I felt the burn in my throat become a little less intense. Then I felt myself start to roll backwards.

"H….."I said. I meant to say hey, but my mouth wouldn't speak all the words I wanted it to. The effects were wearing off faster than I thought!

I rolled and rolled until I hit something. It was thick and solid. It was like a rock. My throat wasn't scratchy anymore, and I could start to speak.

"Ouch…" I managed. "Where…I..?"

It was slowly getting better as I tried to speak.

"HELLO?!? ANY…OUT THERE…!" I yelled.

I didn't get an answer. I could move my arms now. I felt around, for something to tell me where I was. My fingers only felt a rocky surface, and then I felt dirt on my left side. I tried to grab the edge of the rock, and pull myself towards the dirt. When I tried to move, I was rolled over some more. I rolled to a wall.

"Where the heck am I?!" I said. I could now fully speak.

My eyelids could move, but only enough for me to squint. My vision was blurry, but I could see the outline of where I was. It was a solid concrete room. There was a small light giving off heat in the center. How did I get from that cave to here?! More importantly, what is this place? I thought there was only blackness and a few trees here and there… I was starting to move my legs. My eyes opened up just a little bit more, and when I looked at the light, I could open them fully and see everything. I couldn't move my legs fully yet, but I could move my head, arms, and eyes. I dragged myself underneath the light. It felt so warm. I closed my eyes and looked at the light. It felt so great. It was freezing in that dark place outside since there was no sun. The ground was cold, and I don't know where it came from, but there was always a chill breeze. I could move my legs after being under the light for a while. I stood up. Now, I was getting a little hungry, but I didn't see a way out.

"Alright, where's the door?" I said, cheerfully.

I couldn't find one.

"Maybe the walls move?" I said to myself.

Nothing would budge.

"Maybe it's the light…" I said, touching it. The light burned my finger.

"Ouch!" I said.

It was getting hotter. Soon, the bulb turned from a warm yellow to a slight orange.

"Okay, I've seen enough; where is the door." I said.

I tried pushing on the walls and the ground, but nothing would work. The light gave off intense heat, and it was starting to get steamy in the room.

"Am I hallucinating?" I said. I couldn't have been though, that light clearly burned my finger.

The light changed from orange to red. The red started to flicker, almost like…a...fire… I realized it was a fire. The fire burned so bright in the bulb that it broke the glass.

"AGH!" I said, as a piece of burning hot glass melted against me.

I needed to get out of here. The fire was literally crawling on the ceiling. I smelled something burning. The ceiling was started to cave in. That's it! Maybe the rock was flammable. I looked around to find a piece of glass that wasn't fully burnt. I couldn't find one though. The fire was starting to spread to the floor. I tore off a small piece of my shirt and stuck it in the fire above me. It started to burn. I needed to light the wall up before this piece of fabric was gone. I set the piece against the wall. Just before it was burned to just the threads, the wall started to catch fire.

"Yes!" I said in triumph.

The wall burned a hole big enough to jump through. There was only one problem. Around the hole was a ring of fire. I was going to have to jump through a hoop of flames. I couldn't touch the sides at all, or I would get burned. I didn't have much time; the roof behind me was just a wall of fire. If I was going to make it out of here I had to jump, right now. I didn't get a running start, but I jumped through the center, only scorching my pants a little.

"HA! TAKE THAT ROOM OF...WALLS...OF…concrete…." I said. "Eh, it doesn't matter."

I ran a little ways and looked around me. I was back in the forest.

"Hmmm…" I said to myself.

Was I dreaming, hallucinating, or was that all real? I'm not sure… it was probably hallucinating; I need some food. I followed a glow coming from my left, and I was back at the tree where the boy took me in the first place.

CHAPTER 26: OTTO

I looked up in the tree and saw a glowing orb. I heard meows again. I was fed up with this guy, and wanted to set some things straight. So, I started to climb. This tree was really old, judging by how tall it was, and how ancient the trunk looked. I almost missed where he had made his little bed at. It was on a thick and sturdy branch. All that was there was a blanket, a bunch of leaves put together forming a pillow, and a box with meows coming from the inside. I opened the box up and inside was a kitten. She was adorable, and she was hungry. I saw a bone she had been knawing on, but now she was starving!

"Oh, look at you!" I said, picking her up. "You need food!"

I remembered that cats can't eat too many oak leaves, or they will get severely sick. I thought I couldn't leave her here to starve, so I put her back in her box and climbed down the tree. I smelled mint on my way here. I ran right outside of the forest, and there was a small patch of mint plants. I picked up a few leaves and ran back to the tree. When I got to the branch, I opened the box and gave the kitten a few leaves. I had 3 for myself and I gave 3 to her. I was starving, so I ate my really quickly. She ate hers, reluctantly. I don't think she liked the smell, but she was hungry. What else was she supposed to do?

I put the kitten back in her box and put a branch on top so she wouldn't go anywhere. I looked around at the tree. Maybe, there was some more food stashed somewhere. I climbed up the tree a little further looking for a hole in the trunk, but I couldn't find one. The only hole in the tree was near the bottom. It was empty. The boy must have gone somewhere. Since he wasn't here, I decided I would wait for him. I don't think he would mind if I kept his place warm for him. I climbed back up the tree and got underneath the thin blanket. It didn't keep me super warm, but it was warmth I was more than willing to take. I laid my head on the makeshift leaf pillow, and closed my eyes. I didn't exactly sleep, but I got to rest. Everything was quiet, except for the wind. It's funny; I would have usually heard some sort of snarl or even a scream… I wasn't complaining though. I did NOT realize how tired I was. Running around, escaping death multiple times, and trying to see in the dark was hard work! I was out before I could say the next sentence I was thinking.

When I woke up, there was a boy on the branch above me. He was a little bit small. He was a little bit skiddish.

"AGH!" I screamed.

"AGHH!" He screamed.

What a wimp!

We caught sight of each other; screamed again and I proceeded to fall off the branch and onto the ground.

"OUCH!" I exclaimed!

"Hey, you're that girl I rescued earlier!" He said.

I started to climb back up the tree.

"Hey, uh… sorry about leaving you for the creatures…" He said, his tone getting a little frightened as I made my way up the tree.

I made my way to his branch.

"Okay, slow down, I didn't mean to--" He said, but I cut him off.

"I'm going to ask you a few questions. A simple yes or no will suffice. 1: Who are you? 2: You saved me, but you let the monsters take me. Why? 3: What were those creatures? 4: I was in a room on fire. Out of nowhere I came to be in this room. How did I get there and what was that place?" I asked.

"First of all, my name is Otto. Second, I thought you were dead. Third, I actually am not entirely sure myself. Fourth, where were you when you entered this place? If you can't tell me where you were I can't tell you what it was." He replied.

I backed down a little. Even though this guy seemed small and dorky, he had some power to him as well.

"I'm Perrie." I said. "When the creatures dragged me off, they bit me with their gums. I think the gums administer some sort of poison because I went blind, and was paralyzed. I couldn't see anything until I had been in the cave for a while. It was still blurry. I was dragged through a thistle patch, and I was brought into a cave. I was then rolled over, multiple times, into that room where I was almost killed."

"Tell me exactly what happened in the room." He said, with a serious look on his face.

"I'm not sure if it was real or not…" I said.

"No, no that's okay, just tell me what happened. I'm curious." He said.

"Okay, so I was rolled into the room. When my vision came back fully, I was in a solid, concrete, square-shaped room. On the ceiling in the center of the room was a light. Something was giving off heat, and it turned out to be the light. I rolled underneath it because I was cold. I was warmed up very quickly. In fact, it was too quick. The bulb started to change color; it went from a soft yellow to orange, and the room got hotter. The light then turned red, and started to flicker. It was a fire. The fire got so hot it exploded the light bulb. A piece of hot glass melted on me. Also, I'd burned my finger earlier because I touched the light. The fire then started to spread. I had no way of escape. I found out that the rock walls were flammable, and decided to burn a hole in the wall. I didn't know what was on the other side, but it had to be better than where I was at the moment. Since the rock was extremely flammable, and the ceiling started to cave in. I ripped a small piece of my shirt off, and waited for it to catch fire. When it did, I put the cloth onto the wall, hoping it would spread. It did, and a hole burned through the wall. I then had to jump through the ring of fire, and I was back where I was before. So, I don't know if I was dreaming or hallucinating; I was really hungry and tired." I said.

"Interesting." He said.

"How so? It wasn't even real!" I said.

"Oh believe me; I don't think you were dreaming." He said.

"What tells you that?" I replied.

"I've heard someone say that before. You're not the only one to have this happen to you. She wasn't in a room with fire though; it was a room with ice." He said. "That girl was a little crazy though. She ran off before the week was over."

"You knew her?" I said.

"I fed her. I never got her name." He said. After hesitating a few moments, he added "You should probably go to sleep. You're very tired, I can tell."

"How do I know you're not going to kill me in my sleep or something..?" I said.

"Hey, you seemed dead. I'm sorry." He said.

"Well, I'm sleeping a few branches below you." I said, making my way down the tree.

I found a branch that seemed to have a little defect in it. It was a hollowed out branch, like a hammock, but strong and spacy. This was a weird tree. I got inside the little hollow space and curled up into a ball. I was freezing.

Before I went to sleep, I realized that I hadn't recharged my spark. I must have been low on energy, but I didn't feel depleted. When I was under that light, it felt almost as if the warmth was charging it. Maybe that's why it felt so great… I fell asleep with these thoughts on my mind.

CHAPTER 27: NIGHTMARES IN A NIGHTMARE

I was back in the house. I felt the woman's arms around me once again. She was sleeping. I started to speak. This time, I could make out a few words, but the rest was muffled.

"…Can I… Want dolly! Dolly…" I said, holding a doll. I was playing with her arms.

"Jessica…" The woman said, stroking my doll's hair.

"Ha-ha!" I said, laughing. I was still small, but I wasn't a toddler.

I heard loud booms that seemed right outside our door. The woman clutched my doll's hair and stopped moving. The booms got even louder!

"Ah!" I said, screaming.

The woman grabbed my hand, and we ran towards a back door. We ran past a body of a man lying on the floor. The woman looked away from it when we passed him. She shoved the back door open, and picked me up. She put me on her shoulder and I was able to look back. I saw a black cloud, chasing us and covering everything in its path. I started to cry.

"Shh! It's okay." The woman said, trembling with fear as well.

We ran as fast as we could, but the cloud was faster. Soon, it engulfed both of us. It was quite a wave of power that hit us. The woman threw me out of her hands. I hit the ground, and all I saw was ash and dust. Everything was black. The ashes were black, the houses were black, the people were covered in black dust, and the ground was covered in black dirt. I was mouthing a name, but I couldn't hear it. It was muffled. I saw a figure run towards me. It was the woman, covered in black ashes. Just when I thought I was going to be safe in her arms, that we could get away from this place, the second explosion came.

CHAPTER 28: OTTO THE JERK

I woke up and I was in a cold sweat, again. I thought those nightmares were over!! I'm already suffering from a living nightmare, and now I have to have a nightmare within a nightmare?! This is all so tortuous. I couldn't see much, but I saw a dim light coming from another orb on Otto's branch. Wait, Otto has an orb!?

"Hey! Otto!" I yelled.

I saw the outline of his face look down at me.

"What?" He said.

"You had another orb and you weren't going to share?!" I asked?

"I was! I was using it to watch you sleep!" He said.

"Yea, that's not creepy at all…" I said. Otto was a creepy dude…

"No, you misunderstand! I was just making sure you were safe and you weren't dead!" He said.

"Yeah, like that automatically makes spying okay." I said, sarcastically.

"Well sorry for trying to be a considerate friend…" He replied.

We're friends? This creep thought we were friends?! He noticed my hesitation to speak...

"Well...uh... I thought we were....but if you don't want to be, fine! See if I care!" He said. "If we're not friends then you can get out of my tree!"

"Fine!" I said. What a jerk.

I climbed out of the tree and onto the ground.

"Sayonara, jerk!" I said. That seemed a little mean, but I was just being truthful...

"To you as well!" He yelled back.

I stomped my way towards the forest.

CHAPTER 29: MISTAKE
Otto

I didn't mean to make her upset. She overreacted a little though. I was reconsidering the slight feelings I had for her and her beautiful face. If her personality is like that all the time… well… this ship has sailed! I lied. I couldn't stop thinking of her. She was so pretty. Underneath her jerky shell, there was a really sweet girl. I could tell. I saw it in her eyes. I know that look because my mother had the same thing. Before she was sentenced to death in the Gloam, she was really tough and strict. Whenever we got into the Gloam though, she cared for me and loved me. She always had loved me, but she didn't show it until she needed to. Maybe I need to get Perrie to show it. That would be tough…but I think I could manage it one day. One day, far away.

I sat in the tree for a while and took Bo out of her box. She had been eating leaves…mint leaves?

"Who brought you these?" I asked her, petting her purring chest. Her purrs actually came from her throat, but they rippled all through her tiny body.

Mint leaves weren't poisonous to cats, so this person knew what they were doing. I don't know anyone besides me and Perrie who have gotten past the beginning and into the real Gloam… was there someone I didn't know about? It's possible. I mean, I don't have any cameras to watch who gets through the beginning; so, how am I supposed to know? I knew there was a small mint patch near the forest, but I was only going to resort to that in emergencies. The only person near the forest at the moment was Perrie. Maybe she found my tree and found Bo, then found the mint patch. Maybe she fed her! Did Perrie really have a heart to do that? Again, there is that loving and caring person on her inside; I just need to get her to show it.

I heard a few shouts coming from the forest. It was Perrie. I heard a couple of them, and I think most of them were meant for me.

"STUPID… WHY ARE YOU SUCH A JERK…?" She yelled. I heard a tiny hitting sound, and then heard her say, "Ouch!"

I heard a snarl, and got to the edge of my branch. I heard a few more muffled things, and then I heard Perrie scream. Yeah right, I'm going to go and rescue her, after what she said to me. I'm kidding, I can't just leave her. I looked at Bo. She was looking at me. I took out the only food I had, a whole Brid, and gave it to her. I put her box in the hole in the trunk, where she could jump up and down safely, but a predator could not. I gave her the Brid.

"Now listen. I might not be back for a while. Stay safe." I said. I wasn't a sucker for animals and I still don't understand why this one captured my heart so easily. She mewed. "I'll be right back. Stay." I knew she would die alone. I felt too bad to leave her here. I could either go and save Perrie, or save the kitten. I looked back at the forest where Perrie was. I was going to try something. I imitated the snarl noise the creatures make. I heard a muffled, "WHAT WAS THAT?!" coming from Perrie. She was okay. I couldn't take care of this kitten much longer, but I knew what I was going to do. I grabbed my orbs and blanket and stuffed them into my bag. I took Bo out of her box, and jumped off the tree. It was a ways down, and I had to hold Bo above my head so she wouldn't get hurt. Once we landed, I held on to her and ran. There was one place that I had never told anyone about. It was the place I found her. I ran to the side of my tree and kept going until I hit a wall. It wasn't very far, maybe about 5 minutes west. Or, what seemed west to me. I felt along the side, and I found it. There was a rock here this time. I took it out of the hole, and some sunlight came in. I heard people above me. They weren't Officials, and I knew they would take care of her. I took Bo and shoved her outside the hole. I heard multiple snarls behind me. Once she was outside, I heard her meow, and heard someone say something about a kitten.

"Her name is Bo." I whispered, and put the rock back across the hole.

I heard the snarls come very close, and I slowly went the other way. They went away after I moved. I took out one of my orbs and turned it to the brightest setting. I could see where my tree was, and everything else within a mile radius. I saw the creatures briefly, running towards my orb, but I turned it off before they could get to me. I ran towards my tree. I made it in about 3 minutes, running fast. I couldn't exactly tell how long it was, but just judging by what it felt like. For all I know, it could have been 5 minutes. Now that Bo was off my mind, I decided to check on Perrie anyway.

When I got to the edge of the forest, something seemed off. One of the trees were lying flat on the ground, knocked over. I looked around for the source of the fallen tree, but I couldn't find a stump large enough that could've hosted this log with leaves. I made my way towards where Perrie sounded, and found more trees like the one in front. They were all either chopped down, or they just seemed to be like that. It was very strange.

I found a small cave, with snarls coming from the inside.

"That must have been where Perrie went to that room." I said to myself. Maybe she wasn't crazy. I mean, I was close enough to try the same steps she did, to see if I could get inside the room.

I went to the cave, but didn't enter, just in case those creatures were inside. I felt on the ground, looking for a rocky surface. A short distance from the cave, I hit a rock. I was a big stone just sitting in the open for no reason! I sat there for a few seconds, and then I began to roll. I was rolled on my back about 5 times before I came to a stop. I felt something go around my hands and feet, and I was dropped over a cliff. I almost screamed, but I hit the ground first. It was a solid ground, concrete almost. The walls were concrete also. I was in the room. The only difference was that there was no light bulb in the center. There was a hole. It was like a sinking hole. I tried to move, but I then realized I was sinking. My hands and feet were tied with rope, I was lying on my side, and the ground was sinking with me on top of it. I was lying in quicksand.

CHAPTER 30: CHAMBER OF DEATH

I remembered from my schooling in the Pure City that quicksand is one of the many things you could find outside the city. It is a dangerous death trap and it was not to be touched. They said if you touched it you were positively going to die. They never really explained how to get out of it. The sand wasn't moving very fast and it was just sand, so I decided to try and stand up. That was a bad idea. The sand was more gripping than I thought. It was almost like a vacuum. When it got close, you would try to run away, but it was too powerful and it would suck you in. I could NOT move anymore, my hair was starting to sink into the sand. I looked for something to pull me out, but there wasn't anything sticking out of the walls.

"This is it.." I thought to myself.

I lay there for a while, thinking about death. If I was going to die, what was the last thing I wanted to do..? Well, my options are limited, considering I am stuck in a concrete room full of sand. If I wasn't here, I wanted to find the perfect person. She needed to be loving and kind, and I thin k that shyness is cute. I not a fan of the super outgoing people, they annoy me. I like the quiet and down to earth people. If I found such a person, we would raise a family. This girl must have dark eyes, because I have light, and I would love to see a mix in my children. I've always wanted a miniature me to run around the house, playing with whatever he can find, annoying his brother/sister. I would be happy and I could die in peace. That wasn't going to happen, now that I was stuck in this death-hole. My feet were completely under the sand. Was there a bottom to this stuff? Surely there would be something…

After my left arm was underneath the sand, I was thinking about Perrie. Where was she? Was she faring well? Was she dead? Or was she at my campsite stealing all my things…I was going to miss her beautiful brown/gray eyes. They changed color in the light. When the light was on, they looked gray; but when it was off, they looked brown. She was beautiful too. She wasn't scrawny and malnourished like all those people in the Pure City who were considered beautiful. She was normal. I respected her for that. I also respected her for just being different. She had short hair while the rest of the girls had long. She didn't care what she ate while other girls did. My other arm was engulfed in the sand.

I was getting depressed by the time my chest started to sink. I had wasted all this time thinking my last thoughts, while I could be trying to get out of here! There wasn't anything I could do though, and I wasn't going to waste my time whining about it. I was going to die, and I wasn't going to be scared. I didn't fear death. If death were a person, I would walk up to it, stare it in the eye, and say, "Bring it on."

Once my chest was half-way into the sand, I started to sink faster. I positioned myself so my head would go last. My shoulders were sinking quickly.

My neck was in the sand. I was sinking slower now. I looked up and saw my last thing. It was a boring old ceiling. I started to think about the last thing I would ever think about. It was Perrie's face. She was smiling, with her eyes almost sparkling. She was full of joy. Then I thought of her sleeping. She was calm and peaceful. Her eyes were closed and she was away from reality.

I closed mine and sunk away from reality. When I went under the sand, I couldn't see anything, and if I opened my mouth, I would've choked. So, I decided to close my eyes, and hold my breath until I couldn't anymore. I felt sand go into my mouth, and I couldn't breathe. My heart started to beat fast, and I knew this was it. I thought of Perrie again. My body started to fail.

CHAPTER 31: CIVILIZATION IN THE DARKNESS
Perrie

When I had entered the forest, I knew there were going to be some creatures, so I thought it would be best to climb the trees and travel on top of the branches. For some reason, the trees were falling. I was in one of them. When the tree fell, I screamed and heard voices. I was stuck underneath a branch and couldn't move. They weren't voices of a predator, they were human voices. I thought I had completely lost it, until I saw one look at me. They had the same mask as that one boy, Zak, wore on his head. One side had a glowing red eye, and the other had a glowing yellow eye. So, if these people came from the Gloam, where did Zak come from? Did he just happen to have the same helmet, or did he come from the Gloam as well?? If he did, that meant there was a way out of here!

There were only 2 people with the masks. The others had some sort of handkerchief around their mouth. I heard them whisper something to one another. One of the masked people came up to me.

"Oh, thank goodness, I thought I would never get out of this tree!" I said, as the person lifted the branch off of me.

"If you don't mind could you please come with us?" He said, with a whisper in the back of his voice.

"…Sure! Where are we going?" I asked.

He didn't respond. He took me to the rest of the people with the handkerchiefs on their mouths. He handed me a white one.

"Put this on." He said.

I put it on my mouth and tied it in the back.

"Hey, my name is Perrie! It's so nice to finally find some people!" I whispered to the person in front of me.

"Be quiet." She said.

"Why?" I whispered.

"Because I don't want to talk to you!" She said.

I recognized that voice. It was slightly high-pitched, but it had a little raspiness to it. This girl had her hair wrapped up in a handkerchief too. I saw small lightly-colored strands on her neck. Even if we were in pitch black darkness, I could still see small outlines of lightly colored things. She was small, but her muscles were toned.

"You seem familiar… Have we met before?" I asked.

She didn't respond. I tore the handkerchief from her mouth. There were her baby lips.

"Katie." I whispered…

CHAPER 32: REUNION

I hugged her. I thought she was dead.

"I thought you were dead!" I said, tearing up a little. Then I slapped her face.

"Ouch! What was that for?!" She said, rubbing her cheek.

"THAT was for running away from me and making me think you were dead." I said, crossing my arms.

"Okay, calm down. I'll explain what happened later, but for now we need to keep quiet and not draw any attention to ourselves. They are already watching. Pretend to not be interested in talking to me anymore, and just stay behind me." She whispered, pointing to the two people with masks.

The two masked people got in front of the line we were all in. I saw Katie tie up her handkerchief around her mouth again. Where were we going? I looked at the people in front of me. These weren't just strangers; these were the people I entered the Gloam with. What was going on?! We started to walk forward. I saw the two masked people pull out orbs, but these were funny looking. They threw them into the air, and I saw a lightning bolt flash across the sky, all the way to the east. They turned us, and we started to follow the bolt. We followed it until it struck the ground in front of us. It was a long and boring walk. I didn't like speaking anyway, but I had so many questions to ask Katie. I really thought she had died. Where did she go, and how did she get down here? What happened? What did she run into?! My mind was spinning again. I was the type of person who liked to learn, and when I had questions, they needed answers. Sometimes I feel like I'll go insane if I don't get some of them answered. They just sit there, in the back of my mind, to forever haunt me.

When we reached the spot that the lightning struck, the masked people stopped. They motioned for us to walk forward. They didn't budge though. We all obeyed, and walked forward. I got to glance at them before I walked forward. They were watching me. The people in front of me started to disappear, but I was too busy watching the masked people to pay any attention. I put one of my feet in front of the other, but there was no ground. I almost fell, but I caught myself. I looked in front of me, but I couldn't see anything. I looked down at the ground in front of me, and then I saw glowing red and yellow lights behind me. There was no cliff, it was just grass. I felt someone kick my back, and I fell into the secret hole. My face hit a solid concrete ground. I was in the room again, but there were people here this time.

CHAPTER 33: DEATH SIMULATORS EVERYWHERE

The masked men had pushed me into this room. I now had absolute proof I wasn't losing it. These rooms were real. They were chambers of death though! We are already dying in the Gloam by itself, but these chambers too? Who was behind this and what were they up to?!

In the room there was no light bulb, but there was an orb on the ceiling instead. Katie was standing at the very back of the wall; she was frightened. I walked up to her.

"Is there something you're not telling me?" I asked her.

"No. Why?" She replied.

"You seem a little more afraid than everyone else." I said.

"That's because I've been here before." She said.

"What do you mean, you've been here before?" I asked.

"I've been in a room like this before and it had the same orb on the ceiling. I was alone though." She said.

"Wait, so you've been in these rooms too? It's not just me?!" I said, excited and relieved.

"Wait, you've been in these situations too?" She asked.

I heard a rumble, and the room started to shake.

"What was that?" I said.

"That is the start of this room. What's going to happen is that orb is going to start spewing liquid nitrogen. It's a different type of nitrogen; this type turns anything it touches into pure ice. It doesn't leave any human flesh underneath, you become ice. If we don't get out of here, we'll be frozen ice sculptures forever." She said.

Why were there death rooms in a giant death room?! I don't understand.

"Alright, you're still alive, how did you get out of this situation before?!" I asked.

"Well, there was a small rock in one of the corners of the room I was in." She said. "I used the rock to break the walls. The orb would try and shoot at me every 2 seconds, so when it froze one of the walls, the wall became ice; I could break it with the rock."

"Well, maybe if the nitrogen freezes one of the walls again, we can break it into chunks and form a way out!" I said.

"That's a good idea, but what about these other people?!" She said.

"Explain it to the people who will listen and follow." I said.

She clapped her hands really hard, trying to get everyone's attention, but it was mass panic. I looked at the orb, and it was starting to freeze. We didn't have much time. Katie yelled out, but it remained useless. She looked at me and shrugged. I nodded my head. We were going to go through with the plan, even if we couldn't do anything about the other people.

I ran over to Katie and we waited for the orb to start shooting. After about ten seconds, everything turned from mass panic into crazy chaos. I'm not sure if that seemed like a difference, but it was. The orb exploded, but the glass shards were hard as rocks. They hit a few people and they got a few small bruises. The frozen beams hit a girl. She slightly screamed, for it was a cold burn. She looked at everyone in fear, but her expression didn't last long. The beam hit her full body, and she became nothing but a frozen ice sculpture. Everyone backed away from her and the orb in fear. The beam changed its target and started to shoot willy-nilly hoping to get whatever it hit. It tried to hit me and Katie a few times, but we ducked. It almost got my head once! Katie and I kept dodging the beam, and finally it hit the wall.

"Quick! Help me break this wall!" I yelled to her.

"Got it!" She said.

We kicked the wall as hard as we could, but we didn't get much of a crack in it.

"This wall is now pure ice, ice is thick and strong! We're going to need help to break it!" I yelled.

The only way that was going to happen was if we could capture the attention of the panicking others. I looked at what remained of the prisoners. There was a strong and burly looking man, a muscly woman, and a skimpy looking teenager.

"HEY! IF YOU GUYS WANT TO LIVE, BREAK THIS PIECE OF ICE. BEHIND IT IS THE WAY OUT!" I yelled to them.

The teenager heard me. I thought it was a boy, judging by the short hair and broad shoulders, but it was a female. Her glasses she had on were cracked, and her sleek hair was all ruffly now with small traces of ice on the tips. She must have been around the ones who had gotten frozen. She tried to get the attention of the others, but they wouldn't listen. She kicked the woman in the leg, and she paid attention. She explained, and the woman got the man to listen. They all ran across the room as quick as possible.

"Where do we hurt the wall?" The man said. He had a thick accent; he must've descended from the original cities in the North before the Pure City existed!

"Try to break the outside. The middle is going to be the strongest part; it was the center of the beam. The outsides weren't the center target and they shouldn't be as strongly frozen." Katie said.

Two of us went on either side, and I took the teenager with me.

"Whichever side breaks first is the side we'll escape through. Keep moving though, don't stop. The beam is still in the room, and until we get a chance to stall it, it will keep shooting." I said.

Everyone kicked furiously at the wall on each side. There wasn't much luck. We got a small crack on our side, but the other side got it to crack faster. They were stronger on that side anyway. We all ran over to the other side and helped the woman and man to break the ice. I was trying to understand why the beam hadn't shot anyone yet, but then I turned around. Katie's foot had been hit. She never made a sound about it either. Then I realized that she was focusing on her side of the wall. When we went to the opposite side of the room to the other wall, she was about to run.

"NO! KATIE STOP! YOUR FOOT!" I said, but it was too late. She tried to run, and fell on her face. The beam hit her legs, and she was stuck on the ground.

I needed to stop that beam. I ran to the opposite side of the wall and rammed into it. My side may have been hurting afterwards, but I had broken the wall into chunks that you could move and take out. I took a chunk out of the wall and ran back to Katie. Everyone else had escaped and left us.

"Katie, I can get you out of here, but there's only one way I can do it." I said. I had to smash the ice keeping her on the floor.

"If you want, you can do it. It's creepy because I can still feel my legs. I thought they were ice." She said. "Just do it."

I dropped the piece of ice on her legs and feet. I heard a crack. I closed my eyes, not wanting to see the damage I had just caused, but then I saw what happened when I opened my eyes. She got up.

"I guess I was wrong. The ice just covers you." She said.

"Doesn't that mean that those people who got hit with the beam are still alive?" I said. "And we're leaving them behind…!"

"Perrie they're already dying if not dead. Their body can't handle the sudden change in temperature. It's too much for their system." She said.

I think I'm, never going to get over the fact that people die, and there is nothing I can do about it. Is it fair? No. Is it right? No. Maybe it isn't. There isn't anything I can do about it though. The only thing I can do is solve this mystery of the rooms and why this is happening. Maybe I could make a tribute to the ones who were lost. Someday, maybe.

Katie and I ran outside, for surely the masked people would come back, seeing that their room is destroyed. We didn't speak, we just ran. She grabbed my hand.

"…Wha-" I said, but I was interrupted.

"It's just so we don't get separated again. Don't freak out." She said, with an annoyed tone to her voice.

She really was clingy and protective. We kept running until she finally told me to stop. We halted in front of something. It was still pitch black and it was still hard to see, but there was a faint outline of something light colored in front of us. I reached my hand out, to feel if anything was in front of me. I was granted the permission to be acquaintance with the cold, hard ground. I fell on my face. Katie had let go of my hand.

"Ouch…" I said. I was so sick and tired of running and tripping into things…

"What are you doing on the ground? Get up!" She said, pulling my wrist off the ground.

I was perfectly fine wallowing in my foolishness, thank you very much Katie… Once I was off the ground she let go of my hand.

"Okay, you have A LOT of explaining to do." I said.

"Not here." She said.

I had had enough of this running away to "safer places" when THERE WERE NONE.

"NO! I'M TIRED OF RUNNING. YOU'RE GOING TO TELL ME WHAT WE'RE DOING, WHY WE'RE HERE, AND HOW YOU'RE STILL ALIVE!!" I shouted. I think I think that might've come out with a bit more anger in it than I thought, but at the moment it didn't matter. I was tired, frustrated, afraid, and just plain angry.

"Keep your voice down!" She whispered in a shouting sort of way.

"NO! THERE'S NOTHING HERE, JUST ANSWER MY QUESTIONS!" I said.

"Not here!" She said.

"WHY NOT HERE? WHAT'S THE BIG DEAL?" I asked.

"It's complicated." She said. "Just follow me to a safer place, and we can talk."

"You can do what you want, I'm staying here. I know you won't leave me because you need me. You kept searching for me. Surely you wouldn't leave a friend, would you?" I said.

"……No. I wouldn't. All I ask is that you step backwards just once." She responded.

"And why would I have to do that?" I asked.

"You're standing on the edge of a hole. I don't know how deep it is, or how big it is, but I almost fell in myself and I don't want something to happen to you." She said.

I immediately took one huge step back.

"Okay then. I can do that." I said.

"Okay let's get away from here and then we can talk." She said.

"Fine…" I said, slightly annoyed with moving around so much.

She grabbed hold of my hand and we walked to the right.

"Almost away from the hole" She said encouragingly.

"How can you tell that when you can't see anything?" I asked.

"Well the hole has small roots poking out of it; so I feel for the roots until they disappear. Once they're gone, that means the hole is gone too." She said.

That made sense. I felt her go towards the ground, feeling for roots.

"We're safe now!" She said, dragging me to the ground to sit.

I crossed my legs and reached my hands outward.

"I just want to make sure you're there. I hate the darkness here." I said.

She reached her hands out to touch mine.

"Okay, now explain." I said in a stern tone. I was still mad at her.

"Okay. Well you saw me run off into the fog, right?" She said.

"Yes. The guards were going to go after you, but they remembered something, laughed and decided not to." I said.

"Alright, let's pick up where we left off then" She said.

"I ran off into the fog for a while. As I was running I noticed that there were rocks everywhere. As I got farther away from those "mines" I saw that the rocks were getting bigger. Eventually they got so big that they formed a wall. It was impossible to get through. I saw a small opening through two of them, but I wasn't small enough to get inside. So, I tried to move the rocks. I mean, they were big, but that didn't mean I couldn't slide them. It took a little while, but I successfully slid one of the rocks to the side and now the opening was big enough for me to get into. I tried to slip through the opening, but instead, I slipped through a hole in the ground and fell. It turns out that those rocks were all just covering holes to this place. I fell quite a ways; I should've died. Thankfully though, there were trees that I fell into. The impact was still painful, but the branches slightly cushioned my fall. When I climbed down the tree, I met up with some sort of monster. As I was running away from it, I ran into the masked people, and they took me. I found you and here I am!" She said.

"That's it?" I said. "Surely you ran into more… If the Officials knew that you could've moved the rocks, why didn't they come after you?"

"I don't know. Maybe they knew I would fall into this place and that's like a death sentence?" She said.

"Maybe…" I said in a suspicious tone. It didn't seem like Katie just fell here… I think there was more that she wasn't telling me

"So what are we going to do?" She asked.

"About what?" I said.

"This. The darkness" She said.

"It's called the Gloam." I said.

"Oh yeah? Who said?" She said.

I thought about Otto.

"A jerk!" I mumbled.

"Well, what are we going to do?" She said.

"There's nothing that we can do. The only thing for us to do is find out why we are here and what those rooms are." I said.

"Well let's get to work!" She said.

I had been trying to say that all along! Right now I was just a little stumped. We were in pitch black darkness, trying to search for some sort of lead, lost.

"I know. Where are we going to go then?" I said.

"I think we should get back to one of those rooms, or find the masked people." She said.

"What? That's basically asking for death! I'd rather not get killed, thank you very much." I said.

"No, I have a plan." She said.

"Well, before I die, I'd like to know your amazing plan." I said, sarcastically.

"It's simple. First we find the masked people. We let them take us, then one of us goes into the room and one stays behind. The one who waits on the outside is going to question the masked people, and the one on the inside is going to look for a camera or something leading to what the rooms might be. Someone could be planning all of this, and we need to know if they watch what happens in the room." She said.

"The person on the outside will die." I said.

"Why do you say that?" She said.

"Those masked people are large. Not in fat ways, but just plain large. Also, there are two of them. One tiny person against two heavy-muscled people? I don't think it's going to work out." I said.

"Have you got a better plan?" She asked.

"Well…..no…" I said.

"Allright then!" She said. "I'm going to make a lot of noise, it may attract the people." She said. "You watch for their yellow and red glowing masks."

"Okay." I said, standing up. I didn't see anything, it was black as black could get.

I heard some scuffling coming from Katie.

"What are you doing?" I asked her.

"I'm trying to find a tree so I can rustle it and yell from the top. I want to make sure they hear us." She said.

"But what if something else hears us? What if we attract a creature instead?" I said.

She didn't hear me. She had climbed the tree and was shaking it back and forth. I felt the wind blow my hair around. She started to make a lot of noise.

"HELP! HELLO!!! ANYONE OUT THERE?! HELP!!!" She screamed.

"Why are you screaming for help?!" I yelled.

"I have noticed they are attracted to people looking for help!" She yelled back.

She screamed for help again. I saw a faint glow in the distance.

"Hey! I see something glowing!" I said.

"Is it red or yellow?!" She said.

"No! It's white! It looks like more of the glow you see from an orb…" I said.

"DON'T MOVE!" She yelled.

I stood still. I saw the light slowly coming this way. Whoever was holding it started to come towards us faster. It broke into a run.

CHAPTER 34: LOST AND FOUND
Otto

I thought I was about into the sand and die, but I woke up in the middle of the forest with an orb before I suffocated. I must've been dreaming. I ran not too far with the orb, and I think I had found her! There was someone talking to her though. Hopefully she wasn't in danger. I ran towards her, hoping a creature wouldn't spot my orb. I came closer, and saw her outline.

"I'VE BEEN LOOKING FOR YOU!" I yelled.

She ran.

Darn it Perrie…

"WAIT! IT'S ME! PERRIE STOP!" I yelled, but it was too late. She was running and couldn't hear me. I ran after her. I heard some snarls towards the back of me, but I didn't pay any attention.

She didn't run very far because she was hiding under a log. I knew that old trick; I had used it many times myself. When I jumped over the log in my way, I turned around, just to check, and I was right. I found her squished up against it.

"Perrie!" I said.

"…Otto?!" She answered.

"I've been looking for you! I'm so happy you're safe!" I said.

"Why have you been looking for me? I thought we weren't friends anymore!" She said.

"I know, I know. I was being a jerk and I'm sorry. I overreacted. I heard you scream; I just wanted to make sure you were safe!" I said.

"I'm perfectly fine! I don't need you to watch over me!" She said.

"I just…uh…" I said.

"You realize you're ruining our plan, right?" She said.

"What plan?" I asked.

She looked over the log. There was a red and yellow glow in the distance. It was getting brighter as it came closer.

"What's that?" I asked.

"GET DOWN!" She whispered harshly, grabbing my arm and pulling me down. "There isn't any time to explain. Just stay out of my way, and you'll be fine."

I saw her go across the log.

"Perrie!" I whispered, but she didn't hear me.

She was running towards the red and yellow glow. I didn't like the feeling I was getting from all of this, so I decided to follow her at a distance. She was sneaking towards the glow. I hid behind a few trees. Since the glow was getting brighter as it came closer, it was getting easier to see. I saw Perrie's outline moving towards the source of the glow. I saw two human figures come into view. They were both large; surely they weren't women. I saw Perrie go up to one of them. She said something, and they gave her a bandana. She tied it around her mouth, and they started to march off. Just before the glow was out of sight, I saw another figure come down from a tree in front of me and follow them. I did the same, but who was that?

I followed the girl in front of me, who was following Perrie, who was following the people in the line in front of her. That sounded really confusing. The line was marched towards this rock. I felt like I had seen this place before… The masked people pushed the rock aside, and light came shining out of it. They ushered some people inside. Perrie was in that group of people, but she didn't budge. She stood her ground, and when they tried to push her, she fought back. What was she doing?! I ran towards her, and broke up the soon to be fight between her and the masked men.

"What are you doing!?" She said.

"Trying to stop you from doing something stupid!" I said.

"It's not stupid, it was going to work!" She yelled.

"If you would've told me what your plan was I wouldn't be doing this!" I said. "What are you trying to do anyway?"

"Trying to-- WATCH OUT!" She said.

I ducked just in time. The masked men had small dart guns and they were shooting at us. I saw one of the darts hit the ground. I picked it up. It looked like a poison dart. I wasn't sure, but they must have been dangerous if they were shooting us with them. The masked men shot a few more times, then ran off. The rock closed over itself.

"NO!" Perrie shouted. She jumped under the rock right before the opening closed.

"Perrie!" I said, but she was gone.

I saw the girl who was following Perrie come towards me right before the entrance under the rock closed.

"What have you done?!" She said to me.

"I haven't done anything! The masked men ran away and she screamed "NO!!" and then jumped under there." I said.

She looked at me, but I couldn't see what her face looked like; it was getting darker. I saw her run away in the direction of the masked men. I didn't know what to do, so I decided to run off with her.

CHAPTER 35: EYE CAM
Perrie

I fell into the room. Everyone started to stare and watch me. It was slightly creepy.

"I'm okay, just a little scratched." I said, but they didn't stop looking at me. There was an orb on the ceiling again, but it didn't do anything. It was just a light. Everyone kept staring at me.

"Are you guys okay?" I asked, but they didn't respond.

One of them walked up to me.

"Hello…" I said.

She looked me in the eyes, but didn't say a word.

"Why aren't you all afraid of this room? You should be scared and running around, not knowing what to do. Instead you stare at me. Why?" I asked.

They didn't respond. Another one walked up to me. I looked at its eyes this time. I saw what looked like a reflection of a tiny gear. I held the persons face in place so I could take a closer look at his eye.

"You aren't human." I said to the robot.

It didn't reply.

The robot had a camera in his eye. He was watching us.

"Alright, how many more of you are robots?" I asked.

I saw one girl almost say something, but she held it in. A robot stared at her.

"Okay then. Why are you here?" I said.

None of them answered.

"You're the test, aren't you?" I said. "I've figured out that these are like test chambers and once you're put into one, you have to face death. If you cannot stop or escape it, you die. You must be the test."

Nobody answered. I looked at the girl who was about to say something earlier, but she was gone. I looked around, and found her lying on the ground. She wasn't dead; she was still breathing. It looked more of like she was sleeping. Did the robots do this to her?

"What did you do to her?" I asked them.

One finally stepped up.

"We were programmed to help the tired and weak." He said.

"I'm not tired or weak though." I said. "What exactly did you do to her?!"

"We helped her. If you're not tired or weak, you may be released." It said.

"So I can just leave?" I said.

"Yes." One of them said, while the wall revealed a hidden door.

Something about this seems wrong. I don't like it. I walked to the door in the wall. I looked back at them. They were still staring at me. So many questions were buzzing in my head. If escaping from this was this easy, I decided to stay behind and get a few things answered. I walked up to one of the robots.

"Who are you, exactly?" I asked it.

"Unknown." It answered.

"…Okay. Why were you put in here? What is your purpose?" I asked.

"To help the weak and tired." It answered.

I had had enough of this; I ran out the door and I was back at the rock we came through. Those robots must've done something to that girl. I didn't trust them, and I had gotten all the info I was going to get out of them. I think the purpose of them was to drive you to insanity. It was working on me. I wonder if those robots were watching me through their eyes. Or, better yet, someone else was looking through their eyes, using them as a camera. I needed to know who. I also needed to find Katie! I wonder if she ran off after the masked men. She probably did. She's like that.

CHAPTER 36: ENCAMPMENT OF ENEMIES
Otto

We followed the masked men to their campsite. I was expecting around 3 or 4 more masked people at their little campsite, but we were wrong. The only thing we weren't expecting was an actual camp with MORE masked men. There was also the problem of the front gate. It was covered in guards. We saw the masked men show the guards some sort of paper slip, and they were allowed inside. The walls weren't horribly tall and that was good. The only problem is that each of the guards have an orb. They would easily see us coming if we tried to run away.

"Okay, we've followed them and now know where they are, let's go." I said, walking in the opposite direction. She grabbed my arm.

"You're not going anywhere. You got yourself into this." She said.

"I'm sorry, who are you again?" I said.

"I'm Katie. Who are you?" She said.

"Otto." I said.

"What an ugly name." Katie said.

"…Ugly? How is it possible for a name to be ugly?!" I asked.

"Shush. We need to get inside." She said.

"Why do we NEED to? Who knows what's in there?" I said.

"We just need to get inside." She said.

I didn't like this girl. She wasn't telling me something.

She didn't say a word to me about what we were going to do; she started marching towards the front gate. I reluctantly followed. It scared me that she was just walking to the main door. It was surrounded by guards. As we got closer, I knew they could see us, but they didn't do anything. No "call for backup" or "intruder alert" just silence. I stopped. I didn't like where this was going. Katie kept on walking until she was at the front gate's doors. She turned to her side to face the masked person standing there. He (or she) didn't raise a gun or anything. She said something and pointed in my direction. I saw the masked people run towards me; their guns were out.

I shouldn't have trusted Katie. I didn't get very far before someone raised a fence around me. I couldn't escape and the masked people captured me. The fence around me became a glass dome. I saw the glow of their masks come closer to the dome. I felt the ground shift underneath me, and it became glass flooring. I felt like an animal, trapped in a cage, stupid enough to fall for the trap. The masked people picked up the container and brought me to the front gate. I saw Katie standing to the side with an evil happiness on her face. I wondered why she was after me though. I barely even knew her! She didn't know me!

Maybe they weren't looking for me. Maybe Katie was told to lead me here, knowing that Perrie would come searching for me!

"Why her? Why are you after her?" I said.

"We are just performing a test." One of the masked people said. "You are bait for the main test subject."

Yeah, I knew that already.

"Why are you performing a test like this? What are you going to do once she comes…If she comes?" I said.

"That is for us to know and for you to find out." He replied.

They carried my prison inside the camp. Once we were inside, I saw everything. I wasn't the only one who was captured and brought here. There were hundreds more of the same glass prisons positioned next to each other. They stared at me as I was being moved to my spot. The camp was in sort of a hexagon shape. In the front was the gate, and there were tents leading up to one giant tent at the point. The camp was surrounded by a wall of course. There were masked people everywhere. The masked people carrying me set me down next to an empty container.

"Is anyone occupying that container to the right of me?" I asked the masked man.

"No." He answered.

All of these prisons were occupied, why was there an empty one? The masked people left before I got the answer to the question. I sat in my prison cell for a long time. I spent that time observing the camp around me. I saw masked people exchanging guns and what looked like food. I could go for a bite. I looked to the big tent. It didn't look like much, but it felt powerful and ominous for some reason. There was a giant orb at the top of it that lit up the whole camp. It looked like a giant circus tent without the stripes and the clowns and the powdered popcorn covering the ground. Thinking of food made my stomach growl; I was starving.

"Hey! Someone? I'm hungry!" I yelled to whoever would listen.

I saw a masked person notice me.

"Hey you! Can you get me something to eat? I'm famished!" I said.

The masked person walked over to me.

"All we have is soup." He said.

"That's fine." I said.

The masked person went away to the big tent, and came back out with a small bowl of steaming hot soup. I had been starving ever since I went looking for Perrie. I don't even remember how many days it has been since I went looking for her. The masked person set the soup outside my door.

"Well… aren't you going to give it to me?" I asked.

"I'm sorry; I don't have the authority key to open your door, or any of the prisoners' doors for that matter." He said.

He trotted off. It was pure torture seeing that steaming hot soup sit in front of me; I couldn't have one sip of it either.

"Hey! Someone! Open my door so I can have my soup! Please?!" I yelled.

Everyone was busy eating and no-one heard me. Maybe there was a window or something meant for food to come through. I pushed on the glass, but nothing moved. If this was just glass, surely I could get out of here. If they thought I was escaping I could just explain I was simply trying to get to my food. I used all my body weight and hit the glass walls around me. They wouldn't budge. I threw myself onto one wall, but the force of the impact bounced back. The whole prison vibrated. I had gotten one masked person's attention, and they ran over to me. They pulled out some sort of card and used it to open a small invisible slot in the glass. They shoved my soup inside and closed it, and then he/she ran off. I caught my soup bowl just before it spilled.

"Thank you…?" I said.

I drank my soup in less than 2 minutes. I was hungry. They gave me a small bowl too, so I tried to make it last. I think I was also hungry because I forgot to bring pure energy with me. Little did I know that today I would be captured and taken prisoner by people I barely know… I needed to preserve my energy as long as I could. There wasn't much room to lie down in the circular prison, so I slid into a sitting position. I put my head against the back of the cell and closed my eyes. I thought of Perrie again. Hopefully she was still mad at me and wouldn't come looking for me. I only wanted her to be safe. If anything happens, I'd rather have it happen to me instead of her.

Before I fell into an exhausted sleep, I saw a different glow coming from the tent. There were so many masked people in there that the tent itself lit up and had a faint reddish-yellow glow to it. I began to see a different glow come out of it this time though. It was bright and lit up a big spot in the tent. The colors weren't red and yellow, they were green and black. I don't know how it was possible to light up the color black, but whatever this was could. It wasn't a threat to the red-yellow masked people; no-one came running outside. I was disappointed for a second; I thought the glow had come to rescue me. It seemed silly, but in a sea of red and yellow, green and black sounds nice. I heard the masked people cheer. The green and black glow must have been something special. I was too tired to peak my curiosity anymore though, I was sleepy. My eyes shut, and I couldn't remember my dream.

CHAPTER 37: UP A TREE
Perrie

I walked around the forest for a while looking for some sort of glow. I couldn't see anything though, I had no orb and it was a deep blackness. I gave up on looking for Katie or Otto; it wasn't safe to be out here in the open. Creatures and monsters roamed the forest all the time. I couldn't say all day or night because I can't tell the difference down here. I tried to feel around for a familiar place, but I couldn't find anything. I felt like I was going in circles. I would either run into another tree or trip over the twig underneath it. So, I decided to climb a tree. It should be safe up there. I haven't seen any flying creatures. I felt around for the nearest tree then felt for branches. These trees weren't like the ones up top; they didn't have any low branches. I guess I was going to have to try and hoist myself up. I felt for any type of knob or piece of bark sticking out of the tree, but I couldn't find any. I tried a different tree, but I still didn't have any luck. These trees weren't meant for climbing. You know now that I think about it, how did these trees grow? There wasn't any light here… Maybe there was long ago? Maybe these trees grew before this earthen covering was put over it. Why didn't they die though? It was strange, but I couldn't let my mind wander; I heard snarls a little ways away. I went to all the trees I could find, but none of them had anything that would help me climb one.

After searching for what seemed like hours, I gave up. It was impossible to find one. The only tree that I could climb before was Otto's, but I was lost and didn't know how to get to it! I heard a snarl coming from my left. I knew that the creatures were getting closer. They could see in this dark place too. I felt on the ground for a rock. If my theory was correct, all of the rocks housed some sort of room below them. It didn't take long to run into a large one. I kicked and pushed it until it would move, and I was correct. An orb's glow shot out from the room. I quickly jumped in, and pulled the rock as far over the hole as I could. I couldn't shut it fully because I couldn't get a firm grip on the rest of it, so I could still see outside a little bit. I would rather be stuck in something like this than face one of those creatures unarmed.

I waited for the room to start its death trap, but nothing happened. I looked at the orb on the ceiling, but it didn't explode into ice shards or spew fire everywhere. I wondered if there was some sort of mechanism that triggered when you closed the door fully. If that was true that meant there was wiring in the walls. If I could find a way to get to the wiring I could set a trap for the creatures outside! I didn't hear any snarls at the moment, so I decided not to use my brilliant idea yet, but I was going to check and see if I was right first. I needed a way for the trap to start. If I got it to start, I had better chances of breaking/opening the walls so I could see the wiring; that is, if there was any. I could have been wrong.

I stared at the orb for a while, pondering what to do. I thought that since the orb was the trap, I had to find a way to trigger it into starting its simulation. I walked up to it and stood under it. If I found something to break it, it should start. I went back to the small opening to the outside and stuck my hand through it. I felt around until I found a branch. Once I did, I dragged it inside the room, and used the orb as a piñata. I swung at it once and the orb swung back and forth. I hit it again, and I saw a spark go through the ceiling. I hit it once more, and the orb exploded. It didn't start to spew fire or ice though; it revealed a mounted camera hiding inside of it, secretly, this whole time. The camera saw me and turned to look at me. I saw my reflection in the glass lens. I wondered if whoever that was could hear me too.

"Hey! Can you hear me? I have some questions for you!" I yelled at it.

The camera looked at my face. It could hear me.

"Alright, can you speak?" I asked it. It turned its head back and forth. I was guessing that was a no.

"Okay so you can answer yes and no questions, right?" I asked it.

It went up and down.

"Alright. If I ask you questions, will you answer, or will you waste my time?" I asked it.

It didn't move. I was wasting my time.

I walked back to the wall and talked to the camera as I destroyed the wall, using my branch. The wall was surprisingly weak.

"So, these rooms. Are you the one behind the killings going on in these rooms?" I asked it. I didn't hear any movements coming from it.

"Is this place, the Gloam as I've heard it been called, is this where people are disappearing to?" I asked it. Still, no sounds came from it.

"Aren't you worried? I'm breaking you wall. I'm destroying your rooms. I'm asking questions. You seem oddly calm. The only reason you would be this quiet…is... you've already sent enforcements to this location, haven't you?" I asked it.

I turned around to see it move up and down. That was a yes. I had been stupid enough to not pay attention to why it was so silent. I hit the wall as hard as I could with my branch. I saw a small crack appear, so I decided to pick up glass shards from the orb and hit the wall furiously. The wall cracked enough for me to take out loose chunks. I heard small shouts outside the rock. The people the camera sent are almost here. I took out a chunk out of the wall big enough for me to see what was on the inside. I was wrong. There weren't any wires inside the walls. The rooms were controlled elsewhere. That meant someone or something else was behind all of this. This was one big operation and there was probably one person behind it all. I needed to find out whom. I heard the rock above me move. The people were here. I saw red and yellow glows coming from the outside. I didn't have any more time to think; I pulled out the chunks from the wall and formed a hole big enough for me to slip through. I jumped through the hole and ran. I was back outside near the rock, behind it this time. It made sense; I was at the back of the room and so was the hole, therefore I ended up on the back of the rock outside. Interesting. Surely though the masked people saw the hole and wouldn't be far behind me. I ran. As I was running, I saw a faint glow coming from a place over a hill. I ran towards it. Anything that had a glow of an orb in this darkness must have been good. I thought of Otto's tree. Maybe he left his orb there. As I got closer to the glow I noticed it was too bright to be coming from one small orb turned all the way up. It was a much brighter glow. There have been more than one orb in that place. I was walking slowly towards the hill, but I stopped before I got to the top. For one thing, the creatures out here were attracted to light. (Even if they hated it.) For another thing, that was WAY too bright of a light to be just one orb. I didn't know of anyone here in the Gloam that had an orb with them, so it couldn't have been the people who came here with me. I crouched down on the hill and crawled just before I reached the top. I was skeptical of what was on the other side, and if I stood up, whatever was there would have seen me. I peeked over the edge, and I couldn't believe what I saw.

CHAPTER 38: KATIE

When I stood up, she ran to meet me. She was hiding behind one of the fence posts of the giant camp.

"Perrie!" She said, as she ran to me.

"Katie!" I said. "Where's Otto at?"

"He's inside the camp." She answered.

"What is this place?" I asked.

"A place full of people!! People that have survived this awful place. Those masked people that found us earlier? They've been looking for people to take to the camps." She said.

"But what about those rooms?" I asked. "They found us, but they put us in those traps!"

"They only look for the strong… Those traps are evening out the weak. It's really a good thing if you think about it. They are doing them a kindness by putting them out of their misery." She said.

"Katie, they were killing innocent people! Tell me how that is kind! It's murder!!" I said.

"Come on inside the camp, they'll explain everything." She said.

She was lying, I could tell.

"Okay. One more thing though, if Otto is inside the camp, why aren't you in there with him?" I asked.

"He told me to keep a look out for you. If I saw you he told me to bring you inside." She answered.

"Otto told you to come looking for me." I said. Otto wouldn't send someone else, he'd do it himself.

"Yes." She said. She scratched at her nose. She was lying. I had seen people lie before and try to hide it, but she wasn't very good at disguising her deception.

"Okay. One more thing, why did you come here willingly?" I asked her.

"What do you mean here?" She asked.

"The Gloam. You should have been able to jump over a hole in the ground." I said.

"……." She was silent. I knew she was lying.

"Look. Just come inside and I won't have to call for backup. We need you alive Perrie." She said.

"Why me?" I asked.

"He asked for you personally." She said.

"Who?" I asked.

I knew she could never be trusted! The real Katie I saw back above ground was selfish. She would never risk her life to come look for me here in the Gloam! She pulled out some sort of weapon. It had a needle on the end. I was about to run, but she stuck the needle into my wrist. I instantly froze. I could only move my eyes. My mouth was half open, but I couldn't get many words through. I saw Katie pull some sort of thing out of her pocket. She set it on the ground next to me and a glass case came around me. It was rounded at the top and flat on the bottom. It was like someone cut a pill in half, put a floor on one half, and stuffed a person inside. Katie pulled out a compact mirror and flashed it against the orb's light coming from the camp. It looked like she just sent a signal.

"You'll see Otto soon." She said.

"Why? What have you done to him?!" I tried to yell to her, but my mouth didn't make any noise and she had already walked away.

CHAPTER 39: A LAST BREATH
Otto

When I woke up, I saw my skin was literally starting to flake. I looked at a reflection of myself in the glass. I looked like a walking pale pastry. My hair was greasy. I kind of liked it that way in general, but today it just looked like someone stuck a blob of mud on there. My eyes were bloodshot even though I slept well last night. My spark needed to be recharged quickly; otherwise the side effects would get worse. The Officials warned us about the side effects of not recharging your spark. The first thing was pale and flaky skin along with bloodshot eyes and blobby hair. The second thing was a lot of coughing. You would feel horribly sick and weak. The last thing that would happen to you would be the spark leaving you entirely, and you would be left dead. The first stage was starting. I only had about a week and a half. I wondered where Perrie was right now. I was really thankful that she wasn't here. That meant that she was either dead or still out there in the dark. I liked to think she was at my tree. She would be safe there for a little while. Unless, that is, she runs out of food. The poor thing would probably die trying to hunt for something. She would go from predator to prey in less than 5 minutes.

I watched the orbs shift their brightness all day in the dark. I was hoping that's how the masked people told the time, because I didn't know minute from day. Who were these masked people anyways? Were they from the Gloam? Were they the Officials? I had no idea and I don't think I'll ever know. My flaky skin was actually pretty freaky. I could run my hand up and down and feel my skin crumble a little each time. I stopped; I would rather not crumble to my death.

After the orb changed from dim to really bright, I saw a group of masked people run to the front gates. They were let outside into the Gloam. They were probably getting more people to put in the death rooms. When they came back I noticed that I was wrong. They had another glass cell with them. I was hoping it wasn't who I thought it was, but again, wrong. It was Perrie. She looked like she couldn't move.

"Perrie!!" I yelled. I banged on my glass. When I hit it, a strange gas came out of the bottom.

"What's this? This wasn't here yesterday..." I said. The gas made me cough, but nothing else happened.

I saw Perrie be taken out of her glass prison.

"Perrie!" I yelled, but she couldn't hear me.

The masked people who were carrying her inside the camp took hold of her arms. Another masked person came out, but he/she had something in his hand. It looked like a piece of cloth. The person walked up to Perrie and put the piece of cloth around her mouth. The two masked people let go of her arms. She started to cough and wheeze.

"Perrie!" I yelled. She still couldn't hear me.

She fell to the ground, still coughing just a little, but then she went limp. One masked person came over to her with a bag. He (or she, I still can't tell the difference,) put her in the bag and tied the top. I heard the people say something into a piece of glass. The glass lit up and there was a face on it. I didn't hear what they were saying to it, but I heard enough. The only thing that I heard was, "dead."

Perrie was dead. I had failed at trying to protect her. Granted, there wasn't much I could do here in the camp, but she wouldn't have run away from me if I hadn't been such a jerk to her. I only wanted to keep her safe. She was a decent human; she didn't deserve to die. I loved her, but she didn't love me back. She never did. She never would.

CHAPTER 40: MYSTERIOUS ENTERTAINMENT

Perrie

The masked people carried me into the camp. There were a lot of tents surrounding this giant on at the back. I looked around and saw some more glass pill prisons around me. They were all occupied except for one. I found that Otto was in the very last one on the left.

"Otto! Hey Otto!" I yelled, but I then realized he wasn't sitting on the floor, he was sleeping. There were slight remains of what looked like a smoke inside his cell.

"What happened to that prisoner?" I asked one of the masked people.

He didn't respond.

They carried my prison inside the big tent. I looked back at Otto, lying on the floor. I hoped he was okay… The masked people set me to one side of the tent. The tent was filled with red/yellow glowing masked people. They all looked at me as I was set in my spot.

When the masked people carrying me set me in the certain spot, a button rose out of the ground. They pressed it, and my glass prison disintegrated. A new and larger one enclosed itself around me. Everyone in the tent started to cheer. I felt the ground below me shake. The prison started to move, and I was taken along with it. The cell moved to the center of the tens, and stadium stands rose around me. I saw the masked people run to take a seat. I didn't like what was happening. Whatever this was, it was for their entertainment and it looked like I was the main feature. Once the people were sitting in their seats, another glass dome came over me and the small space in the middle of the stands. My glass prison disintegrated again. An orb came out of the glass above me. I DID NOT like where this was going at all. I had a fluttery feeling in my stomach. The orb on the top of the glass dome turned from bright white to gray. It was darkening. As the orb got darker, so did the inside of the glass. Soon, the orb turned black and everything was dark. It was just like the outside of the Gloam. I heard cheers coming from the outside of the glass. I heard a whistling kind of sound. It was like the sound you get when you brew tea and it's finished. I saw a glow coming from the orb on the ceiling. When I looked up at it, it turned from white to a bright green. What was going on?

CHAPTER 41: OPPOSITES
Otto

When I woke up, I saw that the glass of my prison was cloudy. That gas did much more than make me cough. When I woke up, I asked about where they took Perrie.

"HEY? SOMEONE! WAS THAT GIRL DEAD? THE GIRL WHO WAS TAKEN TO THIS CAMP RECENTLY?" I asked to whoever would listen.

I saw a masked person turn to my cell. He or she shook her head side to side. Wait, does that mean no? Perrie wasn't dead. Why would I have seen that? Did that gas that was administered into my cell do more than just make me cough? Was I dreaming or hallucinating…? Either way, I didn't have time to pay attention. That flaky skin wasn't a hallucination; I was entering stage 1 of not having a spark recharged. The Officials never really had a name for the process. I would just call Deterioration, because really, that's all it was. I had about a week to get rid of it.

I looked at my skin. It literally looked like a crumbly pastry that was slowly reducing to nothing. I was afraid to touch it; it looked so fragile. I saw my reflection in the glass prison again. My eyes were still bloodshot, but some of that was seeping into my actual pupil. There were rumors that in stage two of (I'll just call it Deterioration.) Deterioration, one of your eyes would become red because it would be so bloodshot. I was getting close to entering stage two.

"Hey! One of your prisoners here is sick! Since you have the dignity to talk to them and feed them, why not heal them as well? I'm dying! You've kept me alive and I think you need me alive!" I yelled to the nearest masked person.

He or she looked at me, and then just ignored me entirely. I couldn't seem to figure out what these people were up to! Some were helpful, others were mean, and others seemed lost. I sat down in my cell again. The Officials never taught us how to survive the Deterioration.

If Perrie wasn't dead though, where was she? Was she really here? I saw a lot of people flock to the main tent a while ago, but surely she wasn't there. It must have been something else. I have to think back. Was the hallucination drug the one responsible for me thinking Perrie was here? It was definitely responsible for me thinking she was dead, but was she actually here? Alive? I did see a group of masked people run out the gates before the gas filled my cell up. Maybe she was here.

"Hey, anyone! Why are you all going to the tent?" I asked the nearest masked people.

One of them looked at me. They made weird buzzing noises, and then their glowing, masked eyes went from red and yellow to black and green.

"..Wait. What..?" I said to myself.

I saw a black and green glow coming from the tent before I went to sleep… Did their masks change colors? I looked around to other masked people and saw their masks were changing color too. I looked at the red and yellow glow that usually came from the tent, but it wasn't yellow and red this time; it was turning black and green. There was only one glow coming out of the tent that was red and yellow. There was always that one masked person who did the opposite… Why? What was going on?

CHAPTER 42: TEST
Perrie

I heard a muffled voice that sounded like it was in my head. I thought I was going crazy after being in all this darkness.

"You are going to be put through a series of tests. If you wish to live, survive. If you do not perform well, you will see nothing but darkness." It said. It had a voice that was like a mix of a male and female. Some parts sounded like a man, others like a woman. It had a robotic tone either way.

I heard what sounded like a bass drum in music. It echoed all across the black dome around me. I heard a metallic clank from my right. At first it was only one, but then I heard more of them. I started running to the other side of the dome. I heard cheers outside. The dome lightened enough for me to see the glows of the people's masks, but they weren't red and yellow. They were green and black. I only saw one that was red and yellow still. The red and yellow glows were for seeing in the dark and detecting life forms. What were the green and black for?

I heard all the cheers from the crowd go silent for a moment. I looked around in the black dome, but I didn't see anything come into view. The metal clanks finally stopped. This time it got much hotter inside the dome. I started to sweat. I saw a faint glow chasing me from behind. It wasn't just a glow from an orb or a light though, this was much worse. I turned around and saw a wall of fire, rocks, and water all mashed up into one. I felt strong winds push me to the ground.

"These are the elements of the earth. Survive, and you will earn an answer." The voice said. It was more feminine this time instead of masculine.

How was I supposed to survive this?! I had been through several of these death tests before, but I didn't have them all at once! In those situations I could see too, which was helpful. This was crazy!

I turned around to face earth's wrath behind me. This was just all a test. Maybe I was supposed to show if I was brave enough to stare death in the face. I've read it before in my only book; it was one of the tales. It was about a girl whose family had been taken by a villain, and the only way she got them back was sacrificing herself for them to live. It turns out the villain let her go for being so honorable about dying. Maybe I had to do the same. I stopped and looked at the wall. It got much scarier as it got closer. I got a fluttery feeling in my stomach. Maybe I wasn't supposed to do this. My mind told my body to run, but I told it not to. I felt the heat of the fire against my face. I felt the sprinkle of the cold water on my hands. I saw small rocks flying towards me. They got bigger as the wave came closer. The wind had blown me to the ground. The wave was about 10 feet away. I was about to scream, but I told myself not to. They could see me on the outside and if I was going to die, I was going to look good. I ruffled my hair for the last time, and closed my eyes.

CHAPTER 43: TICKING TIME BOMB
Otto

As I was trying to figure out what was going on inside the tent and with the people's masks, I started to cough. It was small and insignificant at first, but it quickly grew into a wheezing cough. How long had I been down here in the Gloam and in this camp? Surely stage two couldn't have started! Maybe I just didn't notice when the flaking of my skin first started. I was too busy worrying about Perrie and the people in the cells around me to notice… I needed to find out what was going on inside that tent. I'm sure Perrie was here. If she WAS here that must have been where she would be. Katie said they needed her for something… I just don't understand what. If they were hurting her in any way, when I get my hands on them…

I really should've been paying attention to the people in the cells around me. I saw the same gas that was administered to me a few days ago still withering in their cells. I couldn't tell if they had just barely gotten it filtered into their cells or not. It was just cloudy in some of them. In a few of them, the first few cells, the gas was different colors. When the gas finally cleared from some of the cells, I saw some people coughing, some starting to fall asleep, and I saw the ones in front start to talk to themselves. I couldn't' hear exactly what they were saying, but they seemed to be yelling at something or someone. My vision wasn't the best far away, but all of them had extremely dilated pupils. I got rid of my glasses because they were becoming a burden. Granted, they helped me to see, but it was no use down here in the Gloam. There was no need for far away visuals, because there was nothing but darkness out there.

The people in the first cells seemed to be going crazy. One of them started to twitch and talk to the ground. It was a little disturbing to watch. I saw gas seep into the first cells again. It was white this time, and looked almost like smoke. Once the gas cleared, they were all lying or sitting on the floor, sound asleep. I looked at the cells closest to me, and they had a grey gas going into their cell. I didn't get to see the effects of it because a black gas seeped into my cell. It clouded my vision, and I couldn't see anything but darkness. I held the sides of my cell pill pod (or whatever it was) and calmed myself down. These gases weren't just appearing out of nowhere. Someone had planned when these would be released into our cells. The person must have been here inside the camp. If they weren't, that meant they were watching from afar. I couldn't see any cameras though, so I wasn't sure. I would believe that they are here more than they aren't.

Once the gas finally parted and my vision was restored, I saw more masked people run into the giant tent. I heard some cheers and I heard what sounded like a soft yell. It wasn't' the robotic yell of the masked men though; it was Perrie's. Or, at least it sounded a lot like her… I put my ear against the glass and listened again. I heard another yell. It was DEFINETLY Perrie. I needed to get out of here! She sounded like she was in trouble. She still doesn't like me, and may not even want my help, but that won't stop me.

I knew the glass wouldn't break by just hitting it, and I wasn't strong enough to do that anyway. I had some muscle, but I wasn't like a Hercules or anything. The gas was coming from somewhere. It was controlled by a person someplace in the camp or someplace far away. Maybe if I could find a way to malfunction the flow, the masked people would come here seeing something is wrong with my cell, and I could escape! It might not work, but it was worth a shot. I needed some way to block the pipe. I knew how to freeze a flow of water in a pipe, but how was I supposed to block flowing air? I was going to have to make the pipe malfunction somehow, or, I could somehow redirect the flow to go somewhere else. I had no idea to how to make it malfunction mechanically; I didn't think it was possible. So, I decided to I had to reroute the pipe. First of all, I had to find out where the gas was coming from. It always seemed to flow up from the ground, but I needed to be sure. I had to wait until they distributed more.

I got my lunch after a while. It was the usual: just plain chicken broth soup. I slowly sipped on it thinking of Perrie. I had heard a few more shouts in the time I had been waiting for the next round of gas. I thought that she was yelling out in pain, but I discovered I could've been wrong. Once I swore I heard her say "I'm not afraid", but I'm still not sure of anything. This gas had messed with my memory. I could still be hallucinating for all I know…
Hopefully all that black gas did was blind my vision.

Right before I was getting hungry for dinner, the process started. I was looking around at the big tent, bored, when I heard a steam sound come from somewhere outside. I looked to the cells nearest to me, and I saw a white foggy gas come into their cell.

"Yes! Bring it on!" I yelled to the floor of my cell.

Nothing happened.

"Oh come on, don't be scared..." I said to it. I felt weird, talking to the floor. I'd been in here too long.

I looked at the other cells and waited for the gas to clear, but it didn't. It stayed there, clouding up the glass. The glass never cleared. I waited for a long time-I even got my dinner-but still, it never cleared. After I was finished eating, I saw a small pinky colored gas rise up out of the floor into my cell.

"There you are!" I said to it. I got as close as I could to the gas before it started to hurt my eyes, and saw small holes in the ground. I saw small little screws next to what looked like a panel on the bottom of the glass prison. It was really hard to see, it took me while to find it. Once I did though, I knew what it was. I took my fork that was given to me with dinner and unscrewed the screws. I slowly took the panel off, so as to not trigger a security system and saw what I was looking for. Inside the small panel was a switch. It was switched on. This was the remote to the control room of my cell. It was like a Bluetooth. Whoever was controlling my cell had access to it by this switch. I looked at the panel before I removed it and there was a security system. This was built to only be removed once, (during its assembling) and all the times since would end in a boom. There was a small explosive on the inside of the panel. If I had gone and removed it like a crazy person I would have pulled the wires attached to the trigger of the bomb on the panel and get blown to bits. Thankfully, I knew that the switch probably had its own security system as well. If I didn't turn it the right way, I would get electrocuted. It didn't have a "DANGER HIGH

VOLTAGE" sign for nothing. It was meant to fool you. I was going to wait until everyone was asleep or not watching to fool with it. I put the panel back in place and sat back down in the prison.

The pink gas didn't feel like it did anything to me, it actually felt good. It felt like something was tickling my nose. It made me smile and I felt happy. Other than that, there wasn't much else that happened. I looked to the cells beside me. The gas still hadn't cleared. I hadn't seen anyone come look out of one either. I hope those people were okay… I didn't eat much of my dinner; I was too busy thinking about how I was going to escape from here and how Perrie was doing. She was definitely here, and she had been in that tent for a while. I hadn't heard many cheers or seen any more masked people run into the tent since lunch.

I finally saw the gas clear after a LONG time. I had felt so tired. I refused to sleep though, I was absolutely sure I was going to break out of this cell today. Or tonight. I seriously can't tell the difference anymore. It's always black here and there aren't any clocks to tell the time. I looked out to the nearest cells and looked at the people lying on the floor. That gas had been in their cells for a good couple of hours. I was hoping it was healthy. They were just lying there on the floor. They weren't dead though, they were still breathing. The top of their cells had remains of the gas just floating around. I think I understood now. The gas came out of the bottom, and it was sucked back up through the top. Maybe the cells were having some difficulties and that gas was in there longer than it needed to be. It couldn't have been wrong though; there weren't any masked people coming to get the people out of their cells. Then again, I had no idea where the masked people were.

I waited a while longer, just to make sure the masked people wouldn't walk out unexpectedly and catch me escaping. I saw the glows start to change inside the tent. I either had more time than before or I was running out. I still wasn't sure about their masks' color changes. I decided to move forward with my plan anyway. I had kept the fork with me from dinner. I don't even know why they gave us a fork for soup in the first place. The masked person who took my dinner and utensils from me looked a little suspicious at first, and I got worried he would notice a missing utensil, but he scratched his mask and walked away. Thankfully he didn't notice me holding the fork behind my back. I didn't have my jacket anymore; I left it in my tree in Bo's old box. I started to think about Bo again.

I took my fork out of my back pocket of my pants and snuck down to the panel in my cell. I slowly unscrewed the tiny screws and left the panel in its place. I wasn't sure if the person watching me knew I had opened it once, and if he did, he could've reprogrammed the bomb to go off when I opened it. I was trying to think of a way I could remove the panel without triggering anything, but if he seriously did that, there wasn't any way I could get inside without getting blown away! I could either risk my life trying, or I could wait for a different solution. I wasn't an ignorant person. I had a decision, and only one of them was logical…or at least seemed to make sense. I examined the panel once more. I lifted the flap just enough to see under the panel. I saw the small bomb on the lid, and then the switch on the inside of the box. I couldn't tell if it had been reprogrammed or not, unless someone left the computer code lying out somewhere.

The only other bad thing about this bomb is it was a time bomb. It was going to go off anyway, regardless of me defusing it or not. I was worried that ALL the cells had this in them. Eventually all of us could be killed off. I couldn't see the time either; the bombs in this place were different. Up in the Pure City, my father was a Major in the military. There hadn't been many wars in the Pure City, so he basically would sit around the house all day and do nothing. I never really paid d any attention to all the military stuff of the Pure City, so I never really knew what type of Major he was. He hadn't fought any wars in his service, but he was put through training, so he knew the rules. Every person who applied to be in the Pure City's military had to go through a training session. All they would do is learn what it was like to be in the military and then they would go through tests. The tests would involve surviving with no food or water in the middle of nowhere, defusing bombs, and tests of life and death. The life and death tests would put you in a situation where you could choose to live or die, whether it was sacrificing yourself for someone, or jumping off a cliff into the ocean to save yourself. It seemed intense, but my father said they weren't as bad as they seemed. The trainees would also learn about the weapons used by the Pure City's military; that's how my father knew about bombs. There were many types of bombs, but there was one that stood out from them all. It was the Pure City's signature time bomb. The Pure City had a different way of making time bombs. They had a way that would hide the clock from sight, and they had an option to make it invisible. It was the ultimate weapon. You could disguise it as a normal stick of dynamite; when the enemy found it and tried to ignite it, they would be the ones who would end up as pieces of toast. You could also just place it somewhere and turn the invisible option on. No one could detect it and no one could see it. It was great for the Pure City.

There was no possible way I could lift the panel without being blown up. There could have been another bomb under there, invisible, for all I knew. I could take the risk and try it anyway, but I was only going to use that for a last resort. It was a stupid decision. I needed more time, and I didn't have any. I needed to act quickly if I was going to get out of here and find Perrie.

CHAPTER 44: DISINTEGRATED
Perrie

I stood in front of the wall. I was fearless. Nothing could hurt me. (I was just thinking that just in case whoever put me here was monitoring my thoughts.)

"COME ON! WHAT ARE YOU WAITING FOR?" I yelled at the wall.

"Well..?" I said.

I saw the wall come forward. I felt a flame lick my face.

"Ouch..." I said, rubbing the scorched skin.

The wall came around me. I felt its heat. The flames lashed out, trying to reach me, but I ducked just in time. The wall turned into a cyclone, and I was in the middle of it. It was truly scary. The fire and water mixed in such a way that it made dark purple objects... like whirling rocks!! The rocks fell to the ground in an instant and disappeared. I stood with my hands stretched outward as though welcoming my death; but I really didn't want to die; I was just playing it out. The cyclone started to close in on me, and it got as close to my face and body as it could, then it disintegrated. It was pitch black again. I was right; they were looking for honor. At least, that's what I thought... They could have just been changing the test.

"Hey, voice, did I pass the tests?" I asked the female/male voice that appeared first in my head.

No answer. I didn't hear anything from outside the dome either. I walked over the wall of the dome that was closest to me. I knocked on it to listen for any reaction, but I quickly retrieved my hand back. The wall had a slight electric shock to it. I did get one knock in though, but still, no response came from outside. What was happening out there? I hadn't heard any cheers or boos or anything! It was completely silent. Too silent. It was DEAD silent. I swear you could hear a person far away breathing. I didn't like it. It could have just been that whoever was controlling this dome muted the outside noises for me to concentrate on the problem ahead of me. If that was the case, I'd better prepare to think quickly again.

I waited for a few minutes, and I saw a green glow come out of the north side of the dome. Or, at least what looked like the north side of it to me. The green glow got closer, but when I touched it, it didn't hurt me. It didn't hurt me at all. I walked into the green light.

CHAPTER 45: WOODEN HOUSE
Otto

Okay, something was seriously wrong here. I hadn't seen any masked people for about a day now. I know I couldn't tell time for sure, but I knew it had at LEAST been a day. Before I went to sleep last night, (what felt like last night) the glows coming from the giant tent had gone out. There wasn't any noise; it was just like they fizzled off without a trace. I was hoping nothing had happened to Perrie. If the masked people had gone somewhere, I was going to have to rearrange my whole entire rescue plan. It wouldn't work if I couldn't get a masked person to come check out the "technical difficulties" in my cell.

I hadn't seen any gas fill up my cell or the cells around me. I wondered what was happening…? I was getting really hungry too; it felt like it was past lunchtime. They didn't feed any of us today either. I saw the other people in the cells around me sitting around, twiddling their thumbs. If I could find a way to communicate with them, maybe we could all devise an escape plan together. I never really like working with other people. Most of the ones I would have to work with were idiots. I just can't stand people who can't figure out a simple problem! It's not that hard! Then again, I was way ahead of my class. I always got picked on by other guys. They would take my glasses and throw them on the ground, calling me childish names. I was never cool. I still don't think I am. Another reason I got rid of my glasses was just to try and impress people I met. Girls don't like guys with glasses…

I was getting lost in my thought and I needed to focus on the situation that confronted me now. How was I going to get out of here and save Perrie? I still had my fork with me from the last meal I had, but I'm not sure if that was going to do me any good considering that the panel could have been rigged with a bomb. The bomb was a time bomb too; it could go off at any given moment. I needed to take that chance of the bomb possibly going off if I opened the panel again. It was a stupid decision, but it had to be done if I wanted to get out of here quickly.

I took the fork out of the back pocket of my pants. I unscrewed the miniatures screws for the third time, and slowly lifted the panel. I could die. This could be last thought. I lifted the panel all the way and thought about Perrie. I really did think I was going to die, but thankfully, nothing exploded. I looked where the time bomb used to be, but I think the person who was controlling my cell made it invisible. I looked at the switch. If it was electrical, it couldn't be at very high voltage. The switch was too small to be covered in dangerous electricity. Like a fool, I wasn't thinking, and turned the switch the other way. I felt a sharp shock go all through my body and all I saw was black.

I woke up in a wooden house. I was in my bed. It was sunny outside. When I got out of my bed, the wooden floorboards creaked. I got up and went into the hallway. I saw that the room I was in was on the far end of the house. The hallway had 3 doors. There were two on the right, and one on the left. I looked behind me, and my bedroom door was at the very end of the hallway. I walked into a large room that had a torn up couch, and completely destroyed table. It was sliced in half. I saw a woman and a child, cowering in the corner of the room.

"Mom!" I yelled.

She said something, but I couldn't make out what it was. I heard a boom in the distance. The ground shook. She motioned for me to take the child she had with her.

"Take Penelope and run! This is the worst they've ever been. I thought I could come back, and we would be safe, but I was wrong. It's my fault and I need to distract them. I'll catch up with you in a while." She said. She hugged me and Penelope. "I love you."

"I love you too. Be safe." I said.

I ran out the door, carrying Penelope on my shoulder. She was tall for her age. I looked behind me and saw a black mushroom cloud. I started to run, but I wasn't fast enough. The force of the explosion pushed both me and Penelope to the ground. I saw a cloud covering everything in its path; it was getting closer. I had dropped the little girl when the shockwave pushed us both to the ground. I grabbed her hand just before the cloud smothered us in its darkness.

CHAPTER 46: UNLOCKED

I woke up on the ground, breathing heavily. I felt my heart beat and it was beating furiously. I haven't had any nightmares in ages! I thought that stage of my life was over. I guess I was wrong. I rubbed my forehead; I had a headache. When I looked at the grass around me, I saw it had been burned. I realized that I wasn't in my cell. I sat up, and saw that everyone's cell had exploded. There were small pieces of glass lying in places, but it wasn't anything that could hurt someone. I didn't see any of the other people who were in the cells around me. I only saw a glimpse of one, but he was running back into the Gloam. There weren't any guards in at the front gates; you could walk right through! I stood up and looked at all the remains of the cells. I saw the metal bases that kept our cell in place still at their original spots. Everything else was destroyed. It was funny though, the exploded cells hadn't done any damage to the surrounding scenery. The tents were still in shape, the campfire the masked people had going hadn't moved, and the chair I saw a masked person sitting in yesterday was still in its place!

After I was through sight-seeing, I ran to the big tent. I needed to get to Perrie before anything else happened. The tent wasn't going to be as easy to get through as I thought. When I got to it, the front had a padlock and chains covering the entrance. I couldn't see inside, the chains were blocking everything from view. I was going to have to cut through these things if I wanted to get inside. I took the fork out of my pocket just to try something. I stabbed the fabric around the chains, to see if it would rip. The fabric was pretty much like steel though; the fork bounced off the tent and I heard a metal bang. Well, THAT was a useful waste of my time.

I tried to think of a place where I could find something sharp enough to cut through these chains. I knew that a mere knife wouldn't do the job. I needed something stronger, more powerful. I felt the chains. They weren't ALL steel, thankfully, but they were more of like a park fence. They weren't very heavy and they would be easy to penetrate, but there were a lot of them. I would have to find one place to cut to make sure I got them all.

I decided to go into some of the masked people's tents, looking for some form of wire cutter. In the first tent was just a bed and a blanket. In the next one was a bed, some food, a blanket, and a small glass tablet. I figured looking in these tents would be a waste of time after I looked in the sixth one.

They were all pretty much the same. I ran to the front gate. Maybe they would have something for the guards to use as a weapon that would suffice for a wire cutter. I looked around for a weapons supply. I found one just underneath the watchtower. Inside were weapons galore. If I needed to kill someone, this would be the place to go, but I wasn't that kind of person. I looked for something that would work as a wire cutter, but all I found were glass scissors. These would obviously not work. I didn't know what was on the other side of that chain door either. It could be something hostile. I grabbed a light gun, in case there was something hostile on the other side. I also found a heat shot underneath some ammo. A heat shot comes in a syringe and is used to administer pure heat. It sounds nice, but in reality this heat is burning. I was going to use it on the metal, hoping it would melt through the chains. I stuck the light gun in my pocket, and ran back outside.

Thankfully, nothing had changed in the camp. I had a slight worry that there could be someone waiting for me outside, but no, it was empty as it was before. I ran back to the chains. I had been running A LOT today. I was huffing and puffing, but I took out the heat shot, and successfully administered it to the chains. I saw the chains slowly melt away. I pushed them apart with my hands and stepped inside the tent. I wasn't prepared for what faced me. Inside the tent was nothing. Everyone was gone. There was no Perrie, no masked people, no anyone. It was empty.

CHAPTER 47: DAYDREAMER
Perrie

When I walked into the green light, I felt a strange feeling come over me. I also felt like someone could possibly be watching me. The green light made my chest feel tight and my stomach feel wobbly. It was like that feeling you get right before you get sick, but then it goes back down. I heard the robotic voice in my head again, but it was glitching.

"Go…don't….it's okay…no…." It said. The voice was female then male at the end. The male sounded different for a second though.

I thought I saw something move to my left, but it was just my eyes playing tricks on me. I kept on walking in the green light. It felt like I had gone past the dome's boundaries. I saw a few things materialize out of the green light. I saw a creature like the ones in the Gloam. It wasn't fully dark this time, and I could see everything. I must have been hallucinating. I touched the creature, but it didn't do anything to me at all. It felt so real though, I ran my fingers through its fur. This creature had one red eye and one yellow eye, just like the masked people. It was a mix between a bird and a fox. It was actually quite frightening. The bird part of it had white tips on its wings, but the wings were covered in fox fur.

"Brid-" I heard the voice in my head say, but it was cut off.

I guess this thing was called a Brid. I looked at it again. The Brid had the body and head of a bird, but it had a fox's legs and tail. On its face were fox ears and a fox nose. I touched it again. I realized that the fur was actually feathers that just looked like fur. It was actually quite interesting. I saw the Brid open its mouth and it made a howling/screeching noise. It had many teeth, but they weren't sharp like a carnivore's. They were rounded, which meant they ate plants. I realized I had been walking in place this whole time. I felt like I had been walking forward, but I hadn't moved at all.

I saw another thing materialize to my right; I walked over to it. It was almost like a pterodactyl, but with a cat's tail and eyes. It was pretty. I didn't hear anything come from the inside of my head; I think the voice was glitching. When I touched the pterodactyl, it disappeared.

"Hey! Where did you go?" I yelled.

I saw it appear behind me. It made me jump.

"So you can disappear and reappear? You must be like a magician's rabbit." I said to it. I touched it again, but it didn't disappear. It flew to the front of me.

"Hey, where are you going?" I said, following it.

I followed it all the way into a yellowish light. The green had changed color. I walked into the yellow light and saw the woman from my dreams standing in front of me.

"Who are you? I've seen you in my dreams!" I said.

"Penelope…" She said, stroking my cheek.

"I'm not Penelope, I'm Perrie." I said to her.

She disappeared. Otto materialized in her place. I knew he wasn't real, but seeing him filled me with excitement.

"Otto! I'm glad you're alive! I thought you were dead…" I said, hugging the illusion.

I saw a little girl appear next to him. She was holding his hand.

"Michael, where are we going?" She asked him.

"We are going to get away from this place. I know a safety house we can go to while we wait for mommy." He said to her.

"Who's Michael? He's Otto!" I said to the younger girl.

She looked at me, and then they both disappeared. What was this? Why were my dreams being showed to me in here?

I saw a scene appear in front of me. It then surrounded me. There was a black sky above, the ground was covered in black ashes, and there was smoke seeping from cracks in the ground. I saw a child running with her mother. It was the same child as before, but she was a bit older now. I saw another girl about the same age with her. They were all holding hands, running. I heard the mother say something to the older version of the little girl from before, but I couldn't hear her. There were booms in the distance that muffled everything. I saw a man run up to the woman, tell her something, then run off with the other little girl. She yelled something. I then went into a first person view of the child with the woman. We ran past a woman who was shot in the stomach. This was just like my dream I had had a few weeks ago… I looked up at the woman. She evaporated right in front of me and I saw masked people with red and yellow glowing eyes surround me. The scene disappeared.

I was still running through the yellow light this whole time. I slowed down until I was at a jogging pace. The light around me turned red. Then I saw blackness creeping up from in front of me. Soon, I was running back in blackness. I saw a faint green circle glowing, and I saw a black one. I stopped. I couldn't control my legs anymore. The green and black glowing dots came closer. All the blackness that surrounded me vaporized. I saw a masked person standing in front of me. This mask was different though… It had green and black glowing eyes.

CHAPTER 48: MEET THE MAKER

The room that held me inside with this masked person was poorly put together. It looked like someone just threw a bunch of metal pieces on the walls and nailed them together. I was standing in place, and I had metal cuffs around my feet. I tried to take them off, but they were clamped shut. I looked at the masked person.

"Who are you?" I asked.

It took off his mask.

"The maker of the Gloam." It said.

I was in shock. I couldn't believe what he was.

"You're...not...human...." I said. "But you can speak English...."

"Yes. We learned through the City's volunteers." It said.

This thing had a human looking body, but it was black. It was all black. Its eyes were green and black, just like the mask's eyeholes. Its eyes were squinted a little, but I couldn't see any pupils. It had a skeletal shaped face. It pretty much did look like a skeleton with skin and glowing eyes. It was frightening creature. Its skin looked leathery. I reached out to touch it.

"I wouldn't suggest you do that. It's poisoned." It said.

I quickly retrieved my hand.

"Who are you, exactly." I said, firmly.

"I am just an intellectual being looking for others like me." It said.

"What do you mean? Where am I?!" I asked.

"Let me start from the beginning, Ms. Fitzgerald. The Pure City has never existed. It was all an illusion." He said.

"That's not possible. For one, the Pure City WAS real, I have lived there my whole life! Second of all, my name is Fawn! Not Fitzgerald!" I said.

"That is where you're wrong, Penelope Fitzgerald. The Pure City was merely a place to house the humans. We have been observing you, Ms. Fitzgerald. The "Gloam" is the only real thing out of all of this. Maybe I should just call it by its real name though, Earth." He said.

"What... What do you mean?!" I said. I couldn't have been the girl in my dreams! Could I?

"Yes, you are the girl in your dreams." He said.

He could read my thoughts?!?

"Yes, I can." He said.

I was dumbfounded.

"You are aboard TPC-1. This is the Pure City. You have been in space for most of your life. It's easier for us to live among you in our own climate. You were brainwashed into thinking everything you think you know about the "Pure City"." He said.

"Where are we now then?" I asked.

"We are in the Northern gate." He said, opening one of the metal pieces like a window. I saw more masked people down below us. They were dressing up like Officials.

"All the Officials….Those were you?" I asked.

He nodded his head.

"And the Gloam…all those dreams… YOU MADE EARTH LIKE THAT, DIDN'T YOU?!!?" I yelled.

He nodded his head again.

"We did it to preserve our race. We live in nothing but the dark. Earth was the same size as our planet, and it was easy to kill off most of you." He said.

"Why did you leave some of us alive then?" I asked. "All those dark bombs… those were what made the Gloam…"

"Yes. We left some of you alive to observe you." He said.

"Why?!" I asked.

"We have gone from planet to planet, observing their species. We only leave the intelligent alive." He said. "You, Penelope, have proved that the humans have great potential to be extremely intelligent one day."

"Wait, so those people who were disappearing in the city… were they being sent to the Gloam?" I asked. "The note on my front step…."

He nodded his head. "Patience Penelope, your questions will be answered soon." He said.

"Why were there so many rooms where you could get killed down there then?!" I asked.

"We put humans through every type of test we could think of. We needed to be sure you were intelligent and could handle touch situations. Even in the Pure City you were being put through tests. The robbery, your tree, many things happened right under your nose. I was almost flattered when you started to search for an answer in the Gloam. Penelope, you have passed every test that was available. So did your brother and sister." He said.

"Brother…?" I asked.

"Don't stop thinking Penelope. You know who it is." He said.

It was Otto. Michael was Otto. There was only one other person who had the last name of Fitzgerald.

"Since you have passed every test though, we will leave you to survive." He said.

"…No." I said.

"….What." He said, in an angry tone.

"You killed a lot of people. You killed my father. You killed my mother. I won't let you keep doing this. We refuse your offer. No." I said.

BOOK 2 OF THE EXCITING TRILOGY COMING OUT SPRING OF 2015:

ABOVE

Made in the USA
San Bernardino, CA
05 February 2014